Why was she feeling such a strong attraction to

en.

ce,

The truck had slowed down for traffic again and she took a quick glance over at him, then wished she hadn't when she saw he was gazing at her with those gorgeous dark eyes. "Yes. Why would you think not?"

"You shivered just now."

He had to have been watching her mighty close to have known that. "Just felt a little chill."

"Then maybe I should turn up the heat."

Turn up the heat?

She was feeling hot enough already!

* * *

Breaking Bailey's Rules is part of
New York Times bestselling author
Brenda Jackson's Westmorelands series—
A family bound by loyalty...and love!

Dear Reader,

I knew Bailey Westmoreland's book was special from the moment I began writing it.

Bailey is the baby of the Denver Westmorelands and the partner-in-crime to her cousin Bane Westmoreland. Ever since I introduced those Westmorelands living in Denver, Bane and Bailey were two characters that you just had to watch and try to keep up with. And my readers have.

Bailey had her mind made up about her path in life and where she wanted to go...or so she thought. Then a man by the name of Walker Rafferty arrives in Westmoreland Country and Bailey's life will never be the same again.

Walker is just the type of man Bailey needs, but she's determined to fight her attraction to him. I hope you enjoy seeing the outcome of their showdown.

Happy reading!

Brenda Jackson

BREAKING
BAILEY'S RULES

BRENDA JACKSON

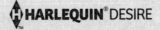

Recycling programs
for this product may
not exist in your area.

ISBN-13: 978-0-373-73420-7

Breaking Bailey's Rules

Copyright © 2015 by Brenda Streater Jackson

Reclaimed by the Rancher
Copyright © 2015 by Harlequin Books S.A.

The publisher acknowledges Janice Maynard for
her contribution to *Reclaimed by the Rancher*.

Printed in U.S.A.

HARLEQUIN®
™ www.Harlequin.com

CONTENTS

Brenda Jackson is a *New York Times* bestselling author of more than one hundred romance titles. Brenda lives in Jacksonville, Florida, and divides her time between family, writing and traveling.

Email Brenda at authorbrendajackson@gmail.com or visit her on her website at brendajackson.net.

Books by Brenda Jackson

HARLEQUIN DESIRE

A Wife for a Westmoreland
The Proposal
Feeling the Heat
Texas Wild
One Winter's Night
Zane
Canyon
Stern
The Real Thing
The Secret Affair
Breaking Bailey's Rules

Visit the Author Profile page at Harlequin.com, or brendajackson.net, for more titles.

BREAKING
BAILEY'S RULES
Brenda Jackson

To the man who will always and forever be
the love of my life, Gerald Jackson, Sr.

Pleasant words are a honeycomb.
Sweet to the soul and healing to the bones.
—*Proverbs* 16:24

Prologue

Hugh Coker closed his folder and looked up at the five pairs of eyes staring at him.

"So there you have it. I met with this private investigator, Rico Claiborne, and he's convinced that you are descendants of someone named Raphel Westmoreland. I read through his report and although his claims sound pretty far-fetched, I can't discount the photographs I've seen. Bart, every one of your sons could be a twin to one of those Westmorelands. The resemblance is that strong. I have the photographs here for you to look at."

"I don't want to see any photographs, Hugh," Bart Outlaw said gruffly, getting out of his chair. "Just because this family might look like us doesn't mean they are related to us. We are Outlaws, not Westmorelands. And I'm not buying that story about a train wreck over sixty years ago where some dying woman gave her baby to my grandmother. That's the craziest thing I've ever heard."

He turned to his four sons. "Outlaw Freight Lines is

a multimillion-dollar company and people will claim a connection to us just to get what we've worked so hard to achieve."

Garth Outlaw leaned back in his chair. "Forgive me if I missed something, Dad, but didn't Hugh say the Westmorelands are pretty darn wealthy in their own right? I think all of us have heard of Blue Ridge Land Management. They are a Fortune 500 company. I don't know about the rest of you, but Thorn Westmoreland can claim me as a cousin anytime."

Bart frowned. "So what if they run a successful company and one of them is a celebrity?" he said in a cutting tone. "We don't have to go looking for any new relatives."

Maverick, the youngest of Bart's sons, chuckled. "I believe they came looking for us, Dad."

Bart's frown deepened. "Doesn't matter." He glanced at Hugh. "Send a nice letter letting them know we aren't buying their story and don't want to be bothered again. That should take care of it." Expecting his orders to be obeyed, Bart walked out of the conference room, closing the door behind him.

Sloan Outlaw stared at the closed door. "Are we going to do what he says?"

"Do we ever?" his brother Cash asked, grinning while watching Hugh put the papers back in his briefcase.

"Leave that folder, Hugh," Garth said, rubbing the back of his neck. "I think the old man forgot he's no longer running things. He retired a few months ago, or did I imagine it?"

Sloan stood. "No, you didn't imagine it. He retired but only after the board threatened to oust him. What's he's doing here anyway? Who invited him?"

"No one. It's Wednesday. He takes Charm to lunch on Wednesdays" was Maverick's response.

Garth's brow bunched. "And where is Charm? Why didn't she attend this meeting?"

"Said she had something more important to do," Sloan said of their sister.

"What?"

"Go shopping."

Cash chuckled. "Doesn't surprise me. So what are we going to do Garth? The decision is yours, not the old man's."

Garth threw a couple of paperclips on the table. "I never mentioned it, but I was mistaken for one of those Westmorelands once."

Maverick leaned across the table. "You were? When?"

"Last year, while I was in Rome. A young woman, a very beautiful young woman, called out to me. She thought I was someone named Riley Westmoreland."

"I can see why she thought that," Hugh said. "Take a look at this." He opened the folder he'd placed on the conference room table earlier and flipped through until he came to one photograph in particular. He pulled it out and placed it in the center of the table. "This is Riley Westmoreland."

"Damn," chorused around the table, before a shocked silence ensued.

"Take a look at the others. Pretty strong genes. Like I told Bart, all of you have a twin somewhere in that family," Hugh said. "It's—"

"Weird," Cash said, shaking his head.

"Pretty damn uncanny," Sloan added. "Makes the Westmorelands' claims believable."

"So what if we are related to these Westmorelands? What's the big deal?" Maverick asked.

"None that I can see," Sloan said.

"Then, why does the old man have a problem with it?"

"Dad's just distrustful by nature," Cash answered Maverick, as he continued to stare at the photographs.

"He fathered five sons and a daughter from six different women. If you ask me, he was too damn trusting."

"Maybe he learned his lesson, considering that some of our mothers—not calling any names—turned out to be gold diggers," Sloan said, chuckling.

Hugh shook his head. It always amazed him how well Bart's offspring got along, considering they all had different mothers. Bart had managed to get full custody of each of them before their second birthdays and he'd raised them together.

Except for Charm. She hadn't shown up until the age of fifteen. Her mother was the one woman Bart hadn't married, but the only one he had truly loved.

"As your lawyer, what do you want me to do?" Hugh asked. "Send that letter like Bart suggested?"

Garth met Hugh's gaze. "No. I believe in using more diplomacy than that. I think what has Dad so suspicious is the timing, especially with Jess running for senator," he said of their brother. "And you all know how much Dad wants that to happen. His dream has been for one of us to enter politics. What if this is some sort of scheme to ruin that?"

Garth stood and stretched out the kinks from his body. "Just to be on the safe side, I'll send Walker to check out these Westmorelands. We can trust him, and he's a good judge of character."

"But will he go?" Sloan asked. "Other than visiting us here in Fairbanks, I doubt if Walker's been off his ranch in close to ten years."

Garth drew in a deep breath and said, "He'll go if I ask him."

One

"Why are they sending their representative instead of meeting with us themselves?"

Dillon Westmoreland glanced across the room at his cousin Bailey. He'd figured she would be the one with questions. He had called a family meeting of his six brothers and eight cousins to apprise them of the phone call he'd received yesterday. The only person missing from this meeting was his youngest brother, Bane, who was on a special assignment somewhere with the navy SEALs. "I presume the reason they are sending someone outside their family is to play it safe, Bailey. In a way, I understand them doing so. They have no proof that what we're claiming is the truth."

"But why would we claim them as relatives if they aren't?" Bailey persisted. "When our cousin James contacted you a few years ago about our relationship with them, I don't recall you questioning him."

Dillon chuckled. "Only because James didn't give me a chance to question anything. He showed up one day at our Blue Ridge office with his sons and nephews in tow and said that we were kin. I couldn't deny a thing when looking into Dare's face, which looked just like mine."

"Um, maybe we should have tried that approach." Bailey tapped a finger to her chin. "Just showed up and surprised them."

"Rico didn't think that was a good idea. From his research, it seems the Outlaws are a pretty close-knit family who don't invite outsiders into their fold," Megan Westmoreland Claiborne said. Rico, her husband, was the private investigator hired by the Westmorelands to find members of their extended family.

"And I agreed with Rico," Dillon said. "Claiming kinship is something some people don't do easily. We're dealing with relatives whose last name is Outlaw. They had no inkling of a Westmoreland connection until Rico dropped the bomb on them. If the shoe was on the other foot and someone showed up claiming they were related to me, I would be cautious, as well."

"Well, I don't like it," Bailey said, meeting the gazes of her siblings and cousins.

"We've picked up on that, Bay," Ramsey Westmoreland, her eldest brother said, pulling her ear. He then switched his gaze to Dillon. "So when is their representative coming?"

"His name is Walker Rafferty and he's arriving tomorrow. I thought that would be perfect since everyone is home for Aidan and Jillian's wedding this weekend. The Atlanta Westmorelands will be here as well, so he'll get to meet them, too."

"What does he intend to find out about us?" Bailey wanted to know.

"That you, Bane, Adrian and Aidan are no longer hellions," Stern Westmoreland said, grinning.

"Go to—" Bailey stopped and glanced at everyone staring at her. "Go wash your face, Stern."

"Stop trying to provoke her, Stern," Dillon said, shaking his head. "Rafferty probably wants to get to know us so he can report back to them that we're an okay group of people. Don't take things personally. Like I said, it's just a precaution on their part." He paused as if an idea had come to him. "And, Bailey?"

"Yes?"

"Since you're the most apprehensive about Mr. Rafferty's visit, I want you to pick him up from the airport."

"Me?"

"Yes, you. And I expect you to make a good impression. Remember, you'll be representing the entire family."

"Bailey representing the entire family? The thought of that doesn't bother you, Dil?" Canyon Westmoreland said, laughing. "We don't want to scare him off. Hell, she might go ballistic on him if he rubs her the wrong way."

"Cut it out, Canyon. Bailey knows how to handle herself and she will make a good impression," Dillon said, ignoring his family's skeptical looks. "She'll do fine."

"Thanks for the vote of confidence, Dillon."

"You got it, Bailey."

Bailey knows how to handle herself and she will make a good impression.

Dillon's words rang through Bailey's head as she rushed into the airport fifteen minutes late. And she couldn't blame her delay on traffic.

That morning she had been called into her boss's office to be told she'd been promoted to features editor. That called for a celebration and she'd rushed back to her desk to call her best friend, Josette Carter. Of course Josette had insisted they meet for lunch. And now Bailey was late doing the one thing Dillon had trusted her to do.

But she refused to accept that she was off to a bad start…even if she was. If Mr. Rafferty's plane was late it would not hurt her feelings one iota. In fact today she would consider it a blessing.

She headed toward baggage claim and paused to look at an overhead monitor. Mr. Rafferty's plane had been on time. Just her luck.

Upon reaching the luggage carousel for his plane, she glanced around. She had no idea what the man looked like. She had tried looking him up online last night and couldn't find him. Josette had suggested Bailey make a sign with his name, but Bailey had rolled her eyes at the idea. Now, considering how crowded the airport was, she acknowledged that might have been a good idea.

Bailey checked out the people retrieving their luggage. She figured the man was probably in his late forties or early fifties. The potbellied, fiftysomething-year-old man who kept glancing at his watch with an anxious expression must be her guy. She was moving in his direction when a deep husky rumble stopped her in her tracks.

"I believe you're looking for me, Miss Westmoreland."

Bailey turned and her gaze connected with a man who filled her vision. He was tall, but that wasn't the reason her brain cells had suddenly turned to mush; she was used to tall men. Her brothers and cousins were tall. It was the man's features. Too handsome for words. She quickly surmised it had to be his eyes that had made her speechless. They were so dark they appeared a midnight blue. Just staring into them made her pulse quicken to a degree that ignited shivers in her stomach.

And then there was his skin tone—a smooth mahogany. He had a firm jaw and a pair of luscious-looking lips. His hair was cut low and gave him a rugged, sexy look.

Gathering her wits, she said, "And you are?"

He held his hand out to her. "Walker Rafferty."

She accepted his handshake. It was firm, filled with authority. Those things she expected. What she didn't expect was the feeling of warmth combined with a jolt of energy that surged through her body. She quickly released his hand.

"Welcome to Denver, Mr. Rafferty."

"Thanks. Walker will do."

She tried to keep her pulse from being affected by the throaty sound of his voice. "All right, Walker. And I'm—"

"Bailey Westmoreland. I know. I recognized you from Facebook."

"Really? I looked you up but didn't find a page for you."

"You wouldn't. I'm probably one of the few who don't indulge."

She couldn't help wondering what else he didn't—or did—indulge in, but decided to keep her curiosity to herself. "If you have all your bags, we can go. I'm parked right outside the terminal."

"Just lead the way."

She did and he moved into step beside her. He was certainly not what she'd expected. And her attraction to him wasn't expected, either. She usually preferred men who were clean shaven, but there was something about Walker Rafferty's neatly trimmed beard that appealed to her.

"So you're friends with the Outlaws?" she asked as they continued walking.

"Yes. Garth Outlaw and I have been best friends for as long as I can remember. I'm told by my parents our friendship goes back to the time we were both in diapers."

"Really? And how long ago was that?"

"Close to thirty-five years ago."

She nodded. That meant he was eight years older than she was. Or seven, since she had a birthday coming up in a few months.

"You look just like your picture."

She glanced at him. "What picture?"

"The one on Facebook."

She changed it often enough to keep it current. "It's supposed to work that way," she said, leading him through the exit doors. And because she couldn't hold back her thoughts she said, "So you're here to spy on us."

He stopped walking, causing her to stop, as well. "No. I'm here to get to know you."

"Same thing."

He shook his head. "No, I don't think it is."

She frowned. "Either way, you plan to report back to the Outlaws about us? Isn't that right?"

"Yes, that's right."

Her frown deepened. "They certainly sound like a suspicious bunch."

"They are. But seeing you in person makes a believer out of me."

She lifted a brow. "Why?"

"You favor Charm, Garth's sister."

Bailey nodded. "How old is Charm?"

"Twenty-three."

"Then, you're mistaken. I'm three years older so that means she favors me." Bailey then resumed walking.

Walker Rafferty kept a tight grip on the handle of his luggage while following Bailey Westmoreland to the parking lot. She was a very attractive woman. He'd known Bailey was a beauty because of her picture. But he hadn't expected that beauty to affect him with such mind-boggling intensity. It had been a while—years—since he'd been so aware of a woman. And her scent didn't help. It had such an alluring effect.

"So do you live in Fairbanks?"

He looked at her as they continued walking. Her cocoa-colored face was perfect—all of her features, including a full pair of lips, were holding his attention. The long brown hair that hung around her shoulders made her eyes appear a dark chocolate. "No, I live on Kodiak Island. It's an hour away from Fairbanks by air."

She bunched her forehead. "Kodiak Island? Never heard of the place."

He smiled. "Most people haven't, although it's the second largest island in the United States. Anchorage and Fairbanks immediately come to mind when one thinks of Alaska. But Kodiak Island is way prettier than the two of them put together. Only thing is, we have more bears living there than people."

He could tell by her expression that she thought he was teasing. "Trust me, I'm serious," he added.

She nodded, but he had a feeling she didn't believe him. "How do people get off the island?"

"The majority of them use the ferry, but air is most convenient for me. I have a small plane."

She lifted a brow. "You do?"

"Yes." There was no need to tell her that he'd learned to fly in the marines. Or that Garth had learned right along with him. What he'd told her earlier was true. He and Garth Outlaw had been friends since their diaper days and had not only gone to school together but had also attended the University of Alaska before doing a stint in the marines. The one thing Garth hadn't done with Walker was remain with him in California after they left the military. And Garth had tried his hardest to talk Walker out of staying. Too bad he hadn't listened.

He'd been back in Alaska close to ten years now and he

swore he would never leave again. Only Garth could get him off the island this close to November, his son's birthday month. Had his son lived he would be celebrating his eleventh birthday. Thinking of Connor sent a sharp pain through Walker, one he always endured this time of year.

He kept walking beside Bailey, tossing looks her way. Not only did she have striking features but she had a nice body, as well. She looked pretty damn good in her jeans, boots and short suede jacket.

Deciding to remove his focus from her, he switched it to the weather. Compared to Alaska this time of year, Denver was nice. Too damn nice. He hoped the week here didn't spoil him.

"Does it snow here often?" he asked, to keep the conversation going. It had gotten quiet. Too quiet. And he was afraid his mind would dwell on just how pretty she was.

"Yes, usually a lot this time of year but our worst days are in February. That's when practically everything shuts down. But I bet it doesn't snow here as much as in Alaska."

He chuckled. "You'd bet right. We have long, extremely cold days. You get used to being snowed in more so than not. If you're smart, you'll prepare for it because an abundance of snow is something you can count on."

"So what do you do on Kodiak Island?" she asked.

They had reached her truck. The vehicle suited her. Although she was definitely feminine, she didn't come across as the prissy type. He had a feeling Bailey Westmoreland could handle just about anything, including this powerful-looking full-size pickup. He was of the mind that there was something innately sensuous about a woman who drove a truck. Especially a woman who was strikingly sexy when she got out of it.

Knowing she was waiting for an answer to his question, he said, "I own a livestock ranch there. Hemlock Row."

"A cattle ranch?"

"No, I raise bison. They can hold their own against a bear."

"I've eaten buffalo a few times. It's good."

"Any bison from Hemlock Row is the best," he said, and didn't care if it sounded as if he was bragging. He had every right to. His family had been in the cattle business for years, but killer bears had almost made them lose everything they had. After his parents' deaths he'd refused to sell and allow Hemlock Row to become a hunting lodge or a commercial fishing farm.

"Well, you'll just have to send me some to try."

"Maybe you'll get to visit the area one day."

"Doubt it. I seldom leave Denver," she said, releasing the lock on the truck door for him.

"Why?"

"Everything I need is right here. I've visited relatives in North Carolina, Montana and Atlanta on occasion, and I've traveled to the Middle East to visit my cousin Delaney once."

"She's the one who's married to a sheikh, right?" he asked, opening the truck door.

"Jamal *was* a sheikh. Now he's king of Tehran. Evidently you've done research on the Westmorelands, so why the need to visit us?"

He held her gaze over the top of the truck. "You have a problem with me being here, Bailey?"

"Would it matter if I did?"

"Probably not, but I still want to know how you feel about it."

He watched her nibble her bottom lip as if considering what he'd said. He couldn't help studying the shape of her mouth and thinking she definitely had a luscious pair of lips.

"I guess it bothers me that the Outlaws think we'd claim

them as relatives if they weren't," she said, her words breaking into his thoughts.

"You have to understand their position. To them, the story of some woman giving up her child before dying after a train wreck sounds pretty far out there."

"As far-out as it might sound, that's what happened. Besides, all it would take is a DNA test to prove whether or not we're related. That should be easy enough."

"Personally, I don't think that's the issue. I've seen photographs of your brothers and cousins and so have the Outlaws. The resemblance can't be denied. The Westmorelands and the Outlaws favor too much for you not to be kin."

"Then, what is the issue and why are you here? If the Outlaws want to acknowledge we're related but prefer not to have anything to do with us, that's fine."

Walker liked her knack for speaking what she thought. "Not all of them feel that way, Bailey. Only Bart."

"Who's Bart?" she asked, breaking eye contact with him to get into the truck.

"Bart's their father," he answered, getting into the truck, as well. "Bart's father would have been the baby that was supposedly given to his grandmother, Amelia Outlaw."

"And Amelia never told any of them the truth about what happened?" Bailey asked, snapping her seat belt around her waist. A waist he couldn't help notice was pretty small. He could probably wrap his arms around it twice.

He snapped his seat belt on, thinking the truck smelled like her. "Evidently she didn't tell anyone."

"I wonder why?"

"She wouldn't be the first person to keep an adoption a secret, if that's what actually happened. From what Rico Claiborne said, Clarice knew she was dying and gave her baby to Amelia, who had lost her husband in that same wreck. She probably wanted to put all that behind her and start fresh with her adopted son."

After she maneuvered out of the parking lot, he decided to change the subject. "So what do you do?"

She glanced over at him. "Don't you know?"

"It wasn't on Facebook."

She chuckled. "I don't put everything online. And to answer your question, I work for my sister-in-law's magazine, *Simply Irresistible*. Ever heard of it?"

"Can't say that I have. What kind of magazine is it?"

"One for today's up-and-coming woman. We have articles on health, beauty, fashion and, of course, men."

He held her gaze when the truck came to a stop. "Why 'of course' on men?"

"Because men are so interesting."

"Are we?"

"Not really. But since some women think so, we have numerous articles about your gender."

He figured she wanted him to ask what some of those articles were, but he didn't intend to get caught in that trap. Instead, he asked, "What do you do at the magazine?"

"As of today I'm a features editor. I got promoted."

"Congratulations."

"Thanks." An easy smile touched her lips, lips that were nice to look at and would probably taste just as nice.

"I find that odd," he said, deciding to stay focused on their conversation and not her lips.

The vehicle slowed due to traffic and she looked at him. "What do you find odd?"

"That your family owns a billion-dollar company yet you don't work there."

Bailey broke eye contact with Walker. Was he in probing mode? Were her answers going to be scrutinized and reported back to the Outlaws?

Walker's questions confirmed what she'd told Dillon. Those Outlaws were too paranoid for her taste. As far as she was concerned, kin or no kin, they had crossed the line by sending Walker Rafferty here.

But for now she would do as Dillon had asked and tolerate the man's presence…and his questions. "There's really nothing odd about it. There's no law that says I have to work at my family's corporation. Besides, I have rules."

"Rules?"

"Yes," she said, bringing the truck to a stop for a school bus. She looked over at him. "I'm the youngest in the family and while growing up, my brothers and cousins felt it was their God-given right to stick their noses in my business. A little too much to suit me. They only got worse the older I got. I put up with it at home and couldn't imagine being around them at the office, too."

"So you're not working at your family's company because you need space?"

"That's not the only reason," she informed him before he got any ideas about her and her family not getting along. "I'm not working at Blue Ridge Land Management because I chose a career that had nothing to do with real estate. Although I have my MBA, I also have a degree in journalism, so I work at *Simply Irresistible*."

She was getting a little annoyed that she felt the need to explain anything to him. "I'm sure you have a lot of questions about my family and I'm certain Dillon will be happy to answer them. We have nothing to hide."

"You're assuming that I think you do."

"I'm not assuming anything, Walker."

He didn't say anything while she resumed driving. Out of the corner of her eye, she saw he'd settled comfortably in the seat and was gazing out the window. "First time in Denver?" she asked.

"Yes. Nice-looking city."

"I think so." She wished he didn't smell so good. The scent of his aftershave was way too nice.

"Earlier you mentioned rules, Bailey."

"What about them?" She figured most people had some sort of rules they lived by. However, she would be the first to admit that others were probably not as strict about abiding by theirs as she was about abiding by hers. "I've discovered it's best to have rules about what I will do and not do. One of my rules is not to answer a lot of questions, no matter who's asking. I put that rule in place because of my brother Zane. He's always been too nosy when it came to me and he has the tendency to take being overprotective to another level."

"Sounds like a typical big brother."

"There's nothing typical about Zane, trust me. He just likes being a pain. Because of him, I had to adopt that rule."

"Name another rule."

"Never get serious about anyone who doesn't love Westmoreland Country as much as I do."

"Westmoreland Country?"

"It's the name the locals gave the area where my family lives. It's beautiful and I don't plan to leave. Ever."

"So in other words, the man you marry has to want to live there, too. In Westmoreland Country?"

"Yes, if such a man exists, which I doubt." Deciding to move the conversation off herself and back onto the Outlaws, she asked, "So how many Outlaws are there?"

"Their father is Bart and he was an only child. He has five sons—Garth, Jess, Cash, Sloan and Maverick—and one daughter, Charm."

"I understand they own a freight company."

"They do."

"All of them work there?"

"Yes. Bart wouldn't have it any other way. He retired last year and Garth is running things now."

"Well, you're in luck with my brother Aidan getting married this weekend. You'll see more Westmorelands than you probably counted on."

"I'm looking forward to it."

Bailey was tempted to look at him but she kept her eyes on the road. She had to add *sexy* to his list of attributes, no matter how much she preferred not to. Josette would be the first to say it was only fair to give a deserving man his just rewards. However, Bailey hated that she found him so attractive. But what woman wouldn't? Manly, handsome and sexy was a hot combination that could play havoc on any woman's brain.

"So were you born in Alaska or are you a transplant?" she asked him out of curiosity.

"I was born in Alaska on the same property I own. My grandfather arrived in Fairbanks as a military man in the late 1940s. When his time in the military ended he stayed and purchased over a hundred thousand acres for his bride, a woman who could trace her family back to Alaska when it was owned by Russia. What about your family?"

A smile touched Bailey's lips. "I know for certain I can't trace my grandmother's family back to when Alaska was owned by Russia, if that's what you're asking."

It wasn't and she knew it, but couldn't resist teasing him. It evidently amused him if the deep chuckle that rumbled from his throat was anything to go by. The sound made her nipples tingle and a shiver race through her stomach. If the sound of his chuckle could do this to her, what would his touch do?

She shook her head, forcing such thoughts from her mind. She had just met the man. Why was she feeling such a strong attraction to him? This wasn't usually how it worked with her and men. Most of the time she thought of them as a nuisance, not an attraction.

"You okay?"

The truck had slowed down for traffic again and she took a quick look over at him. She wished she hadn't when she met those gorgeous dark eyes. "Yes, why would you think I'm not?"

"You shivered just now."

He had to have been watching her mighty close to have known that. "Just a little chill."

"Then, maybe I should turn up the heat."

Turn up the heat? She immediately jumped to conclusions until he reached out toward her console and turned the knob. *Oh, he meant that heat.* Within seconds, a blast of warmth flowed through the truck's vents.

"Better?"

"Yes. Thanks," she said, barely able to think. She needed to get a grip. Deciding to go back to their conversation by answering his earlier question, she said, "As far as my family goes, we're still trying to find out everything we can about my great-grandfather Raphel. We didn't even know he had a twin brother until the Atlanta Westmorelands showed up to claim us. Then Dillon began digging into Raphel's past, which led him to Wyoming. Over the years we've put most of the puzzle pieces together, which is how we found out about the Outlaws."

Bailey was glad when she finally saw the huge marker ahead. She brought the truck to a stop and looked over at him. "Welcome to Westmoreland Country, Walker Rafferty."

Two

An hour later Walker stood at the windows in the guest bedroom he'd been given in Dillon Westmoreland's home. As far as Walker could see, there was land, land and more land. Then there were the mountains, a very large valley and a huge lake that ran through most of the property. From what he'd seen so far, Westmoreland Country was beautiful. Almost as beautiful as his spread in Kodiak. Almost, but not quite. As far as he was concerned, there was no place as breathtaking as Hemlock Row, his family home.

He'd heard the love and pride in Bailey's voice when she talked about her home. He fully understood because he felt the same way about his home. Thirteen years ago a woman had come between him and his love for Hemlock Row, but never again. Now he worked twice as hard every day on his ranch to make up for the years he'd lost. Years when he should have been there, working alongside his father instead of thinking he could fit into a world he had no business in.

But then no matter how much he wished it, he couldn't change the past. Wishing he'd never met Kalyn wouldn't do because if he hadn't met her, there never would have been Connor. And regardless of everything, especially all the lies and deceit, his son had been the one person who'd made Walker's life complete.

Bringing his thoughts back to the present, Walker moved away from the window to unpack. Earlier, he'd met Dillon and Ramsey, along with their wives, siblings and cousins. From his own research, Walker knew the Denver Westmorelands' story. It was heartbreaking yet heartwarming. They had experienced sorrows and successes. Both Dillon's and Ramsey's parents had been killed in a plane crash close to twenty years ago, leaving Dillon, who was the eldest, and Ramsey, the second eldest, to care for their thirteen siblings and cousins.

Dillon's parents had had seven sons—Dillon, Micah, Jason, Riley, Canyon, Stern and Brisbane. Ramsey's parents had eight children, of which there were five sons—Ramsey, Zane, Derringer and the twins, Aidan and Adrian—and three daughters—Megan, Gemma and Bailey. The satisfying ending to the story was that Dillon and Ramsey had somehow managed to keep all their siblings and cousins together and raise them to be respectable and law-abiding adults. Of course, that didn't mean there hadn't been any hiccups along the way. Walker's research had unveiled several. It seemed the twins—Adrian and Aidan—along with Bailey and Bane, the youngest of the bunch, had been a handful while growing up. But they'd all made something of themselves.

There were definitely a lot of Westmorelands here in Denver, with more on the way to attend a wedding this weekend. The ones he'd met so far were friendly enough. The ease with which they'd welcomed him into their group was pretty amazing, considering they were well aware of the reason he was here. The only one who seemed bothered by his visit was Bailey.

Bailey.

Okay, he could admit he'd been attracted to her from the first. He'd seen her when she'd entered the baggage claim area, walking fast, that mass of curly brown hair slinging around her shoulders with every step she took. She'd had a determined look on her face, which had made her appear adorable. And the way the overhead lights hit her features had only highlighted what a gorgeous young woman she was.

He rubbed his hand down his face. The key word was *young.* But in this case, age didn't matter because Kalyn had taught him a lesson he would never forget when it came to women, of any age. So why had he suddenly begun feeling restless and edgy? And why was he remembering how long it had been since he'd been with a woman?

Trying to dismiss that question from his mind, Walker refocused on the reason he was here…as a favor to Garth. He would find out what his best friend needed to know and return to Kodiak. Already he'd concluded that the Westmorelands were more friendly and outgoing than their Alaskan cousins. The Outlaws tended to be on the reserved side, although Walker would be the first to say they had loosened up since Bart retired.

Walker knew Garth better than anyone else did, and although Garth wasn't as suspicious as Bart, Garth had an empire to protect. An empire that Garth's grandfather had worked hard to build and that the Outlaws had come close to losing last year because Bart had made a bad business decision.

Still, Walker had known the Outlaws long enough to know they didn't take anything at face value, which was why he was here. And so far the one thing he knew for certain was that the Westmorelands and the Outlaws were related. The physical resemblance was too astounding for them not to be. Whether or not the Westmorelands had an ulterior motive to claiming the Outlaws as relatives was yet to be seen.

Personally, he doubted it, especially after talking to Megan Westmoreland Claiborne. He'd heard the deep emotion in her voice when she'd told him of her family's quest to find as many family members as they could once they'd known Raphel Westmoreland hadn't been an only child as they'd assumed. She was certain there were even more Westmoreland relatives out there, other than the Outlaws, since they had recently discovered that Raphel and Reginald had an older brother by a different mother.

In Walker's estimation, the search initiated by the Westmorelands to find relatives had been a sincere and heartfelt effort to locate family. It had nothing to do with elbowing in on the Outlaws' wealth or sabotaging Jess's chances of becoming an Alaskan senator, as Bart assumed.

Walker moved away from the window the exact moment his cell phone rang. He frowned when he saw the caller was none other than Bart Outlaw. Why would the old man be calling him?

"Yes, Bart?"

"So what have you found out, son?"

Walker almost laughed out loud. *Son?* He shook his head. The only time Bart was extranice was when someone had something he wanted. And Walker knew Bart wanted information. Unfortunately, Bart wouldn't like what Walker had to say, since Bart hated being wrong.

"Found out about what, Bart?" Walker asked, deciding to be elusive. He definitely wouldn't tell Bart anything before talking to Garth.

He heard the grumble in Bart's voice when he said, "You know what, Walker. I'm well aware of the reason

Garth sent you to Denver. I hope you've found out something to discredit them."

Walker lifted a brow. "Discredit them?"

"Yes. The last thing the Outlaws need are people popping up claiming to be relatives and accusing us of being who we aren't."

"By that you mean saying you're Westmorelands instead of Outlaws?"

"Yes. We *are* Outlaws. My grandfather was Noah Outlaw. It's his blood that's running through my veins and no other man's. I want you to remember that, Walker, and I want you to do whatever you have to do to make sure I'm right."

Walker shook his head at the absurdity of what Bart was saying. "How am I to do that, Bart?"

"Find a way and keep this between us. There's no reason to mention anything to Garth." Then he hung up.

Frowning, Walker held the cell phone in his hand for a minute. That was just like Bart. He gave an order and expected it to be followed. No questions asked. Shaking his head, Walker placed a call to Garth, who picked up on the second ring.

"Yes, Walker? How are things going?"

"Your father just called. We might have a problem."

"I heard Walker Rafferty is a looker."

Bailey lifted the coffee cup to her lips as Josette slid into the seat across from her. Sharing breakfast was something they did at least two to three times a week, their schedules permitting. Josette was a freelance auditor whose major client was the hospital where Bailey's sister Megan worked as a doctor of anesthesiology.

"I take it you saw Megan this morning," Bailey said, wishing she could refute what Josette had heard. Unfortunately, she couldn't because it was true. Walker was a looker. Sinfully so.

"Yes, I had an early appointment at the hospital this morning and ran into your sister. She was excited that the Outlaws had reached out to your family."

Bailey rolled her eyes. "Sending someone instead of coming yourself is not what I consider reaching out. One of the Outlaws should have come themselves. Sending someone else is so tacky."

"Yes, but they could have ignored the situation altogether. Some people get touchy when others claim them as family. You never know the reason behind it."

Since Bailey and Josette were pretty much regulars at McKays, the waitress slid a cup of coffee in front of Josette, who smiled up at the woman. "Thanks, Amanda." After taking a sip, Josette turned her attention back to Bailey. "So tell me about him."

"Not much to tell. He looks okay. Seems nice enough."

"That's all you know about him, that he looks okay and seems nice enough?"

"Is there something else I should know?"

"Yes. Is he single? Married? Divorced? Have any children? What does he do for a living? Does he still live with his mother?"

Bailey smiled. "I didn't ask his marital status but can only assume he's single because he wasn't wearing a ring. As far as what he does for a living, he's a rancher. I do know that much. He raises bison."

"I take it he wasn't too talkative."

Bailey took another sip of coffee as she thought of the time she'd spent with Walker yesterday. "He was okay. We had a polite conversation."

"Polite?" Josette asked with a chuckle. "You?"

Bailey grinned. She could see why Josette found that amusing. Bailey wasn't known for being polite. "I prom-

ised Dillon I'd be on my best behavior even if it killed me."
She glanced at her watch. "I've got to run. I'm meeting
with the reporter taking my old job at nine."

"Okay, see you later."

After Bailey walked out of the restaurant, she couldn't
help but think about Josette's questions. There was a lot
Bailey didn't know about Walker.

She'd remedy that when she saw him later.

Walker was standing in front of Dillon's barn when
Bailey's truck pulled up. Moments later he watched as
she got out of the vehicle. Although he tried to ignore it,
he felt a deep flutter in the pit of his stomach at seeing her
again. Today, like yesterday, he was very much aware of
how sensuous she looked. Being attracted to her shouldn't
be anything he couldn't handle. So why was he having a
hard time doing so?

Why had he awakened that morning looking for her at
the breakfast table, assuming she lived with Dillon and
his wife, since she didn't have her own place? Later, he'd
found out from her brother Ramsey that Bailey floated,
living with whichever of her brothers, sisters or cousins
best fit her current situation. But now that most of her relatives had married, she stayed in her sister Gemma's house
since Gemma and her husband, Callum, had their primary
home in Australia.

He continued to watch her, somewhat surprised by his
own actions. He wasn't usually the type to waste his time
ogling a woman. But with Bailey it couldn't be helped.
There was something about her that demanded a man's attention regardless of whether he wanted to give it or not.
Her brothers and cousins would probably skin him alive if
they knew just where his thoughts were going right now.

The cold weather didn't seem to bother her as she moved
away from the truck without putting on her coat. Dressed

in a long-sleeved shirt, a long pencil skirt that complimented her curves and a pair of black leather boots, she
looked ready to walk the runway.

Squinting in the sun, he watched as she walked around
the truck, checking out each tire. She flipped her hair away
from her shoulders, and he imagined running his fingers
through every strand before urging her body closer to his.
There was no doubt in his mind he would love to sample
the feel of their bodies pressed together. Then he would
go for her mouth and—

"Walker? What are you doing here?"

Glad she had interrupted his thoughts, he replied, "I'm
an invited guest, remember?"

She frowned as she approached him. "Invited? Not the
way I remember it. But what I'm asking is why are you out
here at the barn by yourself? In the cold? Where is everyone? And why didn't you say something when I got out of
the truck to let me know you were over here?"

He leaned back against the barn's door. "Evening, Bailey. You sure do ask a lot of questions."

She glared at him. "Do I?"

"Yes, especially for someone who just told me yesterday
that one of her rules is not answering a lot of questions,
no matter who's asking. What if I told you that I happen
to have that same rule?"

She lifted an angry chin. Was it his imagination or was
she even prettier when she was mad? "I have a right to ask
you anything I want," she said.

He shook his head. "I beg to differ. However, out of
courtesy and since nothing you've asked has crossed any
lines, I'll answer. The reason I'm outside by the barn is because I just returned from riding with Ramsey and Zane.
They both left for home and I wasn't ready to go in just
yet."

"Zane and Ramsey actually left you out here alone?"

"Yes, you sound surprised that they would. It seems there are some members of your family who trust me. I guess your brothers figure their horses and sheep are safe with me," he said, holding her gaze.

"I didn't insinuate—"

"Excuse me, but I didn't finish answering *all* your questions," he interrupted her, and had to keep from grinning when she shut her mouth tightly. That same mouth he'd envisioned kissing earlier. "The reason I didn't say anything when you got out of the truck just now was because you seemed preoccupied with checking out your tires. Is there a problem?"

"One needs air. But when I looked up from my tires you were staring at me. Why?"

She had to know he was attracted to her. What man in his right mind wouldn't be? She was beautiful, desirable—alluring. And he didn't think the attraction was one-sided. A man knew when a woman was interested.

But he didn't want her interest, nor did he want to be interested in her. He refused to tell her that the reason he hadn't said anything was because he'd been too mesmerized to do so.

"I was thinking again about how much you and Charm favor one another. You'll see for yourself when you meet her."

"*If* I meet her."

"Don't sound so doubtful. I'm sure the two of you will eventually meet."

"Don't sound so sure of that, Walker."

He liked the sound of his name from her lips. Refusing to go tit for tat with her, he changed the subject. "So how was your day at work, Bailey?"

Stubbornly, Bailey told herself he really didn't give a damn how her day went. So why was he asking? Why did she find him as annoying as he was handsome? And why, when she'd looked up to see him staring at her, had she felt something she'd never felt before?

There was something so startling about his eyes that her reaction had been physical. For a second, she'd imagined the stroke of his fingers in her hair, the whisper of his heated breath across her lips, the feel of his body pressed hard against hers.

Why was her imagination running wild? She barely knew this man. Her family barely knew him. Yet they had welcomed him to Westmoreland Country without thinking things through. At least, that was her opinion. Was her family so desperate to find more relatives that they had let their guard down? She recalled days when a stranger on their land meant an alarm went out to everyone. Back then, they'd never known when someone from social services would show up for one of their surprise visits.

Knowing Walker was waiting for her to answer, she finally said, "It went well. It was my first day as a features editor and I think I handled things okay. You might even say I did an outstanding job today."

He chuckled. "No lack of confidence on your part, I see."

"None whatsoever." It was dusk and being outside with him, standing by the barn in the shadows, seemed way too intimate for her peace of mind. But there was something she needed to know, something that had been on her mind ever since Josette had brought it up that morning.

Not being one to beat around the bush when it came to things she really wanted to know, she asked, "Are you married, Walker?"

Walker stared at her, trying to fight the feel of air being sucked from his lungs. Where the hell had that question come from? Regardless, the answer should have been easy enough to give, especially since he hadn't been truly married even when he'd thought he had been. How could there be a real marriage when one of the parties took betrayal to a whole new level?

Silence reigned. Bailey had to be wondering why he hadn't answered. He shook off the unpleasant memories. "No. I'm not married." And then he decided to add, "Nor do I have a girlfriend. Any reason you want to know?"

She shrugged those beautiful shoulders that should be wearing a coat. "No. Just curious. You aren't wearing a wedding ring."

"No, I'm not."

"But that doesn't mean anything these days."

"You're right. Wearing a wedding ring doesn't mean anything."

He could tell by her frown that she hadn't expected him to agree with her. "So you're one of those types."

"And what type is that?"

"A man who has no respect for marriage or what it stands for."

Walker couldn't force back the wave of anger that suddenly overtook him. If only she knew how wrong she was. "You don't know me. And since you don't, I suggest you keep your damn assumptions to yourself."

Then, with clenched teeth, he walked off.

Three

The next morning Bailey sat behind the huge desk in her new office and sipped a cup of her favorite coffee. Yesterday had been her move-in day and she had pretty much stayed out of the way while the maintenance crew had shifted all the electronic equipment from her old office into this one. Now everything was in order, including her new desk, on top of which sat a beautiful plant from Ramsey and Chloe.

She couldn't help thinking, *You've come a long way, baby.* And only she and her family truly knew just how far she'd come.

She'd had some rebellious years and she would be the first to admit a little revolutionary spirit still lived within her. She was better at containing it these days. But she still liked rousing her family every once in a while.

Growing up as the youngest Westmoreland had had its perks as well as its downfalls. Over the past few years, most of her family members had shifted their attention away from her and focused on their spouses and children. She adored the women and men her cousins, brothers and sisters had married. And when she was around her family she felt loved.

She thought of her cousin Riley's new baby, who had been born last year. And there were still more babies on the way. A whole new generation of Denver Westmorelands. That realization had hit her like a ton of bricks when she'd held Ramsey and Chloe's daughter in her arms. Her first niece, Susan, named after Bailey's mother.

Bailey had looked down at Susan and prayed that her niece never suffered the pain of losing both parents like Bailey had. The agony and grief were something no one should have to go through. Bailey hadn't handled the pain well. None of the Westmorelands had, but it had affected her, the twins—Adrian and Aidan—and Bane the worst because they'd been so young.

Bailey cringed when she thought of some of the things she'd done, all the filthy words that had come out of her mouth. She appreciated her family, especially Dillon and Ramsey, for not giving up on her. Dillon had even taken on the State of Colorado when social services had wanted to take her, Bane and the twins away and put them in foster care.

He had hired an attorney to fight to keep them even with all the trouble the four of them were causing around town. Because somehow he'd understood. Somehow he'd known their despicable behavior was driven by the pain of losing their parents and that deep down they weren't bad kids.

"Little hell-raisers" was what the good people of Denver used to call them. She knew it was a reputation the four of them were now trying to live down, although it wasn't always easy. Take last night, for instance.

Walker Rafferty had almost pushed her into reacting

like her old self. She hated men who messed around after marriage. As far as she was concerned, the ones who messed around before marriage weren't any better but at least they didn't have a wedding ring on their finger.

Pushing away from her desk, she moved to the window. Downtown Denver was beautiful, especially today, seeing it from her new office. The buildings were tall, massive. As far as she was concerned, no other city had more magnificent skyscrapers. But even the breathtaking view couldn't make her forget Walker's callous remark.

Just like Bailey would never forget the pain and torment Josette had suffered while being married to Myles. Against their parents' wishes the two had married right out of high school, thinking love would conquer all as long as they were together. Within a year, Josette found out Myles was involved with another woman. To add insult to injury, he'd blamed Josette for his deceit, saying that it was because she'd decided to take night classes to get a college degree that she'd come home one night to find him in their bed with another woman. A woman who happened to be living in the apartment across the hall.

That was why Bailey had been so mad about Walker's insinuations that wearing a wedding ring meant nothing to a man. She'd been so angry that she'd only hung around Dillon's place long enough to hug his sons, Denver and Dade, before leaving.

It was obvious that Walker was just as mad at her as she was with him, but she didn't have a clue as to why. Yes, maybe her reaction had been a bit too strong, but seriously, she didn't give a royal damn. She called things the way she saw them. If he hadn't meant what he said, he should not have said it.

The beeping of the phone on her desk got her attention and she quickly crossed the room to answer it. It was an interoffice call from Lucia. Ramsey's wife, Chloe, was the magazine's founder and CEO but it was Chloe's best friend Lucia who ran things as editor in chief. Lucia was married to Bailey's brother Derringer. Although it was nice having her sisters-in-law as first and second in command at the magazine, it also put a lot of pressure on Bailey to prove that whatever accolades and achievements she received were earned and well deserved and not the result of favoritism. Just because Chloe and Lucia were Westmorelands, that didn't mean Bailey deserved preferential treatment of any kind. And she wouldn't have it any other way.

"Yes, Lucia?"

"Hi, Bailey. Chloe stopped by and wants to see you."

Bailey raised an arched brow. What could have brought Chloe out of Westmoreland Country so early today? It wasn't even nine in the morning yet. After marrying Ramsey, Chloe had pretty much decided to be a sheep rancher's wife and rarely came into the office these days.

Bailey slid into her jacket. "Okay. I'll be right there."

Deciding to take the longest route back to Dillon's place, Walker rode the horse and enjoyed the beauty of the countryside. There was a lot about Westmoreland Country that reminded him of Kodiak Island, minus the extremely cold weather, of course. Although the weather here was cold, it was nothing compared to the harsh winters he endured. It was the middle of October and back home the amount of snowfall was quadruple what they had here.

But the differences in the weather weren't what was bothering him today. What bothered him today had everything to do with the dreams he'd had last night. Dreams of Bailey. And that talk they'd had by the barn.

Even now the memory of their conversation made him angry. She'd had no right to assume anything about him. No right at all. She didn't know him. Had no idea the hell he'd been through or the pain he'd suffered, and was still suffering, after almost ten years. Nor did she have any idea what he'd lost.

By the lake, he slowed the horse and took a deep breath. The mountain air was cleansing; he wished it could cleanse his soul, as well. After bringing the horse to a stop he dismounted and stared at the valley below. *Awesome* was the only word he could use to describe what he saw.

And even though he was mad as hell with Bailey, a part of him thought she was pretty awesome, as well. What other way was there to describe a woman who could rile his anger and still star in his erotic dreams? He had awakened several times during the night with an erection. It had been years since that had happened. Not since he'd returned to Kodiak from California.

He had basically thrown himself into working the ranch, first out of guilt for not being there when his father had needed him, and then as a therapeutic way to deal with the loss of Connor. There were some days he'd worked from sunup to sundown. And on those nights when his body had needed a woman it had been for pleasure and nothing else. Passionate but emotionless sex had become his way of life when it came to relationships, but even that had been years ago.

Walker no longer yearned for the type of marriage his parents and grandparents had shared. He was convinced those kinds of unions didn't exist anymore. If they did, they were the exception and not the norm. He would, however, admit to noticing the ease with which the Westmoreland men openly adored their wives, wearing their hearts on their sleeves as if they were a band of honor. So, okay, Walker would include the Westmorelands in the exceptions.

He remounted the horse to head back. Thoughts of Bailey hadn't ended with his dreams. Even with the light of day, she'd invaded his thoughts. That wasn't good.

He had told Dillon he would leave the Monday after this weekend's wedding, but now he figured it would be best if he returned to Kodiak right after the wedding. The farther, and the sooner, he got away from Bailey, the better.

He'd learned enough about the Westmorelands and would tell Garth what he thought, regardless of Bart's feelings on the matter. If Bart thought he could pressure Walker to do otherwise, then he was mistaken.

Walker had nothing to lose since he'd lost it all already.

Bailey walked into Lucia's office to find her sisters-in-law chatting and enjoying cups of coffee. Not for the first time Bailey thought her brothers Ramsey and Derringer had truly lucked out when they'd married these two. Besides being beautiful, both were classy women who could be admired for their accomplishments. Real role models. The two had met at a college in Florida and had remained best friends since. The idea that they'd married brothers was remarkable, especially since the brothers were as different as day and night. Ramsey was older and had always been the responsible type. Derringer had earned a reputation as a womanizer of the third degree. Personally, Bailey had figured he would never settle down and marry. Now not only was he happily married but he was also the father of a precious little boy named Ringo. He had stepped into the role of family man as if he'd been made for it.

Chloe glanced up, saw Bailey standing in the doorway, smiled and crossed the room to give her a hug. "Bay, how are you? You rushed in and out of Dillon's place last night. We barely spoke, let alone held a conversation. How's day two in your new position?"

Bailey returned her sister-in-law's smile. "Great. I'm

ready to roll my sleeves up and bring in those feature sto-
ries that will grow our readership."

Chloe beamed. "That's good to hear. I wanted to con-
gratulate you on your promotion and let you know how
proud I am of you."

"Thanks, Chloe." Bailey couldn't help but be touched
by Chloe's words. She had begun working for the company as a part-timer in between her classes at the university. She had liked it so much that she'd changed her major
to journalism and hadn't regretted doing so. It was Chloe,
a proponent of higher education, who had encouraged her
to also get her MBA.

"So what brings you out of Westmoreland Country so
early?"

"I'm meeting Pam in a little while. She wants me to sit
in on several interviews she's hosting today. She's hiring
a director for her school."

Bailey nodded. Dillon's wife, Pam, was a former actress and had opened an acting school in her hometown of
Gamble, Wyoming, a few years ago. The success of that
school had led her to open a second one in Denver.

Taking her by the arm, Chloe said, "Come sit with us
a minute. Share a cup of coffee and tell me how you like
your office."

"I love it! Thanks to the both of you. The view is simply
stunning."

"It is, isn't it?" Lucia said, smiling. "That used to be
my office and I regretted giving it up. But I have to admit
I have a fantastic view in here, as well."

"Yes, you certainly do," Bailey said, agreeing, glancing around the room that was double the size of her office. When her gaze landed on Lucia's computer screen,
Bailey went still.

"Recognize him?" Lucia asked, adjusting the image of
a face until it took up the full screen.

Bailey sucked in a deep breath as she felt the rapid thud of her pulse. Even if the clean-shaven face had thrown her for a quick second, the gorgeous eyes staring at her were a dead giveaway, not to mention that smile.

"It's Walker Rafferty," she said. He looked years younger, yet his features, sharp and sculpted, were just as handsome.

Chloe nodded, coming to stand beside her. "Yes, that's him. At the time these photos were taken most people knew him as Ty Reklaw, an up-and-coming heartthrob in Hollywood."

Shocked, Bailey looked back at the computer screen. Walker used to be an actor? No way. The man barely said anything and seemed to keep to himself, although she knew he'd formed a pretty solid friendship with her brothers and male cousins.

What had Chloe just said? He'd been an up-and-coming heartthrob in Hollywood? Bailey studied his image. Yes, she could definitely believe that. His grin was irresistibly devastating, to the point where she felt goose bumps form on her arms.

She glanced back at Chloe and Lucia. "He's an actor?"

"He used to be, around ten years ago and he had quite a following. But then Ty Reklaw left Hollywood and never looked back," Chloe said, sitting back down in her chair.

A frown bunched Bailey's forehead. "Reklaw? As in Reklaw, Texas?"

Lucia chuckled as she poured Bailey a cup of coffee. "I doubt it. Probably Reklaw as in the name Walker spelled backward. You know how movie stars are when they don't want to use their real names."

Bailey's gaze narrowed as an idea popped into her head. "Are you sure Walker Rafferty is his real name?"

"Yes. I asked Dillon."

Bailey's brow raised. "Dillon knew who he was?"

"Only after Pam told him. She remembered Walker

from the time she was in Hollywood but she doubted he remembered her since their paths never crossed."

Bailey nodded. Yes, she could imagine any woman remembering Walker. "So he used to be an actor with a promising future. Why did he leave?"

Lucia took a sip of her coffee. "Pam said everyone assumed it was because of the death of his wife and son. They were killed in a car accident."

"Oh, my God," Bailey said. "How awful."

"Yes, and according to Pam it was quite obvious whenever he and his wife were seen together that he loved and adored her. His son had celebrated his first birthday just days before the accident occurred," Lucia said. "The loss was probably too great and he never recovered from it."

"I can understand that." Having lost both her parents in a tragic death a part of her could feel his pain. She reflected on their conversation last night when she'd asked if he was married. He'd said no and hadn't told her he was a widower.

She then remembered the rest of their conversation, the one that had left them both angry. From his comment one might have thought the sanctity of marriage didn't mean anything to him. Or had she only assumed that was what he'd meant? She shuddered at the thought.

"Bailey? Are you okay?"

She looked up at the two women staring at her. "Not sure. I might have offended Walker big-time last night."

"Why? What happened?" Lucia asked with a look that said she wished she didn't have to ask.

Bailey shrugged. "I might have jumped to conclusions about him and his attitude about marriage and said something based on my assumptions. How was I to know he'd lost his wife? I guess he said what he did because the thought of marrying again is painful for him."

"Probably since, according to Pam, he was a dedicated husband and father, even with his rising fame."

Bailey drew in a deep breath, feeling completely awful. When would she learn to stop jumping to conclusions about everything? Dillon and Ramsey had definitely warned her enough about doing that. For some reason she was quick to automatically assume the worst about people.

"Is that why you rushed in and out of Dillon and Pam's place last night? Because you and Walker had words?" Chloe asked.

"Yes. At the time I was equally mad with him. You know how I feel about men who mess around. Before marriage or after marriage."

Chloe nodded. "Yes, Bailey. I think we all know. You gave your poor brothers and cousins hell about the number of girlfriends they had."

"Well, I'm just glad they came to their senses and settled down and married." Bailey began pacing and nervously nibbled her bottom lip. Moments later she stopped and looked at the two women. "I need to apologize to him."

"Yes, you do," both Lucia and Chloe agreed simultaneously.

Bailey took a sip of her coffee as a question came to mind. "If Walker was so hot in Hollywood, then why don't I remember him?"

Lucia smiled. "If I recall, ten years ago you were too busy hanging with Bane and getting into all kinds of trouble. So I'm not surprised you don't know who was hot and who was not. I admit that although I remember him, he looks different now. Still handsome but more mature and definitely a lot more rugged. The beard he wears now makes him nearly unrecognizable. I would not have recalled who he was if Pam hadn't mentioned it. Of course when she did I couldn't wait to look him up this morning."

"Was he in several movies?" Bailey asked. She intended to find any movies he'd appeared in as soon as she left work.

"No, just two. One was a Matthew Birmingham flick, where Walker played opposite actress Carmen Atkins, as her brother. That was his very first. He was hot and his acting was great," Chloe said, smiling. "According to Pam, although he didn't get an award nomination, there are those who thought he should have. But what he did get was a lot of attention from women and other directors in Hollywood. It didn't take him long to land another role in a movie directed by Clint Eastwood. A Western. He'd just finished filming when his wife and son were killed. I don't think he hung around for the premiere. He left for Alaska and never returned."

Bailey didn't say anything. She was thinking about how to get back in Walker's good graces. "I'll apologize when I see him tonight."

"Good luck," Chloe said, chuckling. "When I left this morning, Thorn and his brothers and cousins had arrived for the wedding and you know what that means."

Yes, she knew. There would be a card game tonight. Men only. And she had a feeling Walker would be invited. Then she had an idea. For the past ten years Walker had lived on his ranch on that remote island. He'd indicated last night that he wasn't married and didn't have a steady girlfriend, which meant he was a loner. That made him just the type of man she needed to interview for one of the magazine's spring issues. She could see him being the feature story. She'd wait and share her idea with Chloe and Lucia until she had all the details worked out.

Bailey then recalled that Walker would be returning to Alaska on Monday after the wedding. That didn't give her much time. She looked back down at Walker's photo.

Getting an exclusive interview with him would definitely mean big sales for the magazine.

She took another sip of her coffee. Now, if she could only get Walker to agree.

Four

Walker threw out a card before glancing at the closed door. How many times had he done that tonight? And why was he expecting Bailey to show up at a men-only card game? The main reason was because it was Bailey, and from what he'd heard from her brothers and cousins, Bailey did whatever Bailey wanted to do. But he'd heard more fondness than annoyance in their voices and figured they wouldn't want it any other way.

So here he was, at what had to be close to midnight, in what was known as Dillon's man cave, playing cards with a bunch of Westmorelands. He would admit that over the past three days he'd gotten to know the Denver Westmorelands pretty well, and today he'd met their cousins from Atlanta, which included those living in Montana.

Walker couldn't help but chuckle at Bart's accusation that the Westmorelands had targeted the Outlaws for monetary gain. Walker knew for a fact that wasn't true. Even if their land development company wasn't making them

millions, from the talk around the table, the horse train-
ing business a few of the cousins owned was also doing
extremely well.

"I hear you chuckling over there, Walker. Does that
mean you have a good hand?"

He glanced over at Zane and smiled. "If I did you'd be
the last person to know until it counted."

That got a laugh from the others. In a way, he was surprised at the ease he felt being around them, even those
Westmorelands he'd only met that day. When he'd returned
to Kodiak from his stint in Hollywood, he'd shut himself
off from everyone except the Outlaws and those members
of the community he'd considered family. As an only child,
he wasn't used to a huge family, but he was being educated
about how one operated, Westmoreland-style.

Thorn was telling everyone about the bike he'd just built
for a celebrity. Walker just continued to study his hand. He
could have added to the conversation, since he happened
to know the man personally. But he stayed silent. That was
a life he'd rather not remember.

Walker heard the knock on the door and all it took was
the tingle that moved up his arm to let him know it was
Bailey. The mere thought that he could want her with such
intensity should have frozen him cold, especially after
what she'd accused him of last night. Instead, the opposite
was happening. He had dreamed of her, allowed her to invade his mind all day, and now his body was responding
in a way it did whenever a man wanted a woman.

"Come in," Dillon yelled out. "And whoever you are,
you better be a male."

Bailey stuck her head in the door. "Sorry to disappoint
you, Dil. I decided to check and make sure all of you are
still alive and in one piece. I can just imagine how much
money has been lost about now," she said with a grin as
she stepped into the room.

Walker was the only one who bothered to look up at her. She was gorgeous. Her hair hung like soft waves across her shoulders and her outfit, a pair of jeans and a blue pullover sweater, emphasized her curves, making her look feminine and sexy as hell.

All he could do was stare at her, and then she met his eyes. Bam! The moment their gazes connected he felt something slam into him. He was sure it had the same effect on her. It was as if they were the only two people in the room, and he was glad her family was more interested in studying their cards than studying them.

One of the things he noticed was the absence of that spark of anger in her eyes. It had definitely been there last night. Instead, he saw something else, something that had heat drumming through every inch of his body. Had frissons of fire racing up his spine. Was he imagining it?

"Go away, Bay. You'll bring me bad luck," wailed her cousin Durango, who'd flown in from Montana. He held his gaze steady on the cards in his hand.

"You're probably losing big-time anyway," she said, chuckling, breaking eye contact with Walker to look at Durango. "Another reason I'm here is to rescue Walker." Her gaze returned to Walker. "He's probably tired of your company about now, but is too nice to say so. So I'm here to rescue him."

Walker saw twelve pairs of eyes shift from their cards to him, but instead of seeing even a speck of curiosity, he saw pity as if they were thinking, *We're glad it's you and not us*. Their gazes then returned to their cards.

"We're not stupid, Bay," Zane Westmoreland said, grinning and throwing a card out. "You think you can pump Walker for information about our plans for Aidan's bachelor party. But we've told Walker the rules. What we say in this room stays in this room."

"Whatever," she said, rolling her eyes. "Well, Walker, do you want to be rescued?"

He didn't have to think twice about it, although he was wondering about her motive. "Why not," he said, sliding back his chair. "But it's not because I haven't enjoyed the company," he said, standing and placing his cards down. "It's because I refuse to lose any more money to you guys. All of you are professional gamblers whether you admit it or not."

Dillon chuckled. "Ian is the only true gambler in the family. We're just wannabes. If he was here you wouldn't be walking out with your shirt on, trust me."

Walker smiled. "Can't wait to meet him." He moved across the room toward the door where Bailey stood. "I'll see you guys in the morning."

"Not too early, though," Zane cautioned, throwing out a card. "This game will probably be an all-nighter, so chances are we'll all sleep late."

Walker nodded. "I'll remember that."

"Any reason you felt the need to rescue me?"

Bailey glanced over at Walker as they headed toward the stairs. "I thought you might want to go riding."

"Horseback riding? This time of night? In this weather?"

She chuckled. "Not horseback riding. Truck riding. And yes, this time of night or, rather, this time of morning since it's after midnight. And it's a nice night. At least nicer than most. Besides, there's something I need to say to you."

He stopped walking and held her gaze. "Didn't get all your accusations off your chest last night?"

She knew she deserved that. "I was out of line and jumped to conclusions."

He crossed his arms over his chest. "Did you?"

"Yes, and if it's okay with you I'd like to talk to you

about it. But not here. So if you're up to riding, I know the perfect place where we can have a private conversation."

From his expression she could tell he was wondering what this private conversation would be about. However, instead of asking he merely nodded and said, "Okay, lead the way."

Bailey nodded, too, and then moved forward. Once they made it downstairs she grabbed her coat and waited while he got his. The house was quiet. Everyone with a lick of sense had gone to bed, which didn't say a lot for herself, Walker, her cousins and brothers. But she had been determined to hang around and talk to Walker.

When they stepped outside she saw the temperature had dropped. It was colder than she'd thought. She glanced over at him. "It won't take long for Kent to warm up."

"Kent?"

She nodded, shoving her hands into the pockets of her coat. "Yes. My truck."

He chuckled. "You gave your truck a name?"

"Yes. He and I go a long way back, so we're best buds. I take care of him and he takes care of me." She smiled. "Let me rephrase that. JoJo helps me take care of him."

"JoJo is Stern's wife, right? The mechanic?"

"Yes," Bailey said, reaching her truck. "The best in Denver. Probably the country. The wor—"

"Okay, I get the picture."

She threw her head back and laughed as she opened her truck door. She climbed inside, buckled up and waited until he did the same. "So where are we headed?" he asked.

She looked over at him. "Bailey's Bay."

Walker had heard about Bailey's Bay and had even covered parts of it yesterday while out horseback riding with Ramsey and Zane. He'd been told by Dillon that Westmoreland Country sat on over eighteen hundred acres.

Since Dillon was the eldest, he had inherited the main house along with the three hundred acres it sat on. Everyone else, upon reaching the age of twenty-five, received one hundred acres to call their own. Bailey had decided to name each person's homestead and had come up with names such as Ramsey's Web, Stern's Stronghold, Zane's Hideout, Derringer's Dungeon and Megan's Meadows. She had named hers Bailey's Bay.

"I understand you haven't built on your property yet," he said, looking out the window. Because of the darkness, there wasn't much to see.

"That's right. There's no need. I have too many cousins and siblings with guest rooms at their homes. And then there's Gemma's house that sits empty most of the time since she's living in Australia."

He didn't say anything but figured shifting from guest room to guest room and from house to house would get old. "You do plan to build one day though, right?"

"Yes, eventually. Right now Ramsey uses a lot of my land for sheep grazing, but that won't stop me when I'm ready. I know exactly where I intend to sit my home, and it's far away from the grazing land."

"I bet your place will be a beauty whenever you decide to build." He had seen all the other homes. Each one was breathtaking and said a lot about the owners' personalities. He wondered what design Bailey would choose. Single story that spread out with several wings? Or a two-story mansion erected like a magnificent piece of art? Either one would be a lot of house for one person. But then didn't the same hold true for the house he lived in? All that land and all that house.

"Yes. I plan to make it a masterpiece."

He didn't doubt that and could even visualize the home she would probably build for herself.

"Bailey's Bay was chosen for me and sits next to Zane's

and between Ramsey and Dillon's properties." She chuckled. "That was a deliberate move on my brothers' and cousins' parts since they figured Zane would stay in my business, and Dillon and Ramsey were the only two people I would listen to."

"Are they?"

"Pretty much, but sometimes I won't listen to anyone."

He couldn't help but smile. Bailey was definitely a rebel. That was probably some of her appeal. That, along with her sensuality. He doubted she knew just how sensual she was. It would be any man's downfall when she did realize it.

They didn't say anything for a while, until she brought the truck to a stop. "Here we are."

Thanks to the full moon and the stars overhead he could make out the lake. It stretched wide and endless and the waters were calm. From riding out here with Zane and Ramsey he knew the lake ran through most of the Westmoreland land. "Gemma Lake, right?"

"Yes. Raphel named it after my great-grandmother. I never knew them, or my grandparents for that matter. They died before I was born. But I heard they were great people and they left a wonderful legacy for us to be proud of."

Walker thought about the legacy his own parents, grandparents and great-grandparents had left and how he'd almost turned his back on that legacy to go after what hadn't been his dream but had been Kalyn's dream. Never again would he allow any woman to have that much power over him.

So why was he here? He had been in a card game and Bailey had showed up, suggesting they leave, and he had. Why? Was he once again allowing a woman to make decisions for him?

Walker glanced over at her. She stared straight ahead and he wondered what she was thinking. He looked back at the lake. It was peaceful. He liked being here with Bailey, parked, sharing this moment with her.

He was well aware they were attracted to each other, although neither of them had acted on it. But the desire was there nonetheless. Whenever they were alone there was always some sort of sexual aura surrounding them. Like now.

Even when there were others around he was aware of her. Like that first night when everyone had shown up at Dillon's for dinner. Walker had kept looking across the table at her, liking the sexy sound of her laugh. He had to be honest with himself—he had deliberately waited for her last night, outside by the barn, knowing she would eventually drop by Dillon's house since Zane had mentioned she did it every day.

The effect she was having on him bothered him, which was why he'd changed his plans so he could leave Saturday evening after the wedding instead of on Monday. The last thing he needed was to get involved with Bailey Westmoreland. He would never marry again, and all he could ever offer her was an affair that led nowhere. That wouldn't be good for her and could affect the friendships he'd made with her family.

He glanced over at her. "You said you wanted to talk," he prompted. The sooner they finished the sooner they could leave. Being out here alone with her could lead to trouble.

She looked over at him. He could barely see her features in the moonlight but he didn't need a bright light to know she was beautiful. She had rolled down the window a little and the cold air coming in enhanced her scent. It was filling his nostrils with the most luscious aroma.

But her looks and her scent weren't the issue; nor should they be. He had to remember he deserved better than a woman who could be another Kalyn.

"About last night."

That got his attention. "What about it?"

"I owe you an apology."

"Do you?"

"Yes. I made accusations that I should not have."

Yes, she had, but he couldn't help wondering what had made her realize that fact. "What makes you so sure?"

She frowned. "Are you saying that I was right?"

"No, that's not what I'm saying. You need to do something about being quick to jump to conclusions."

She waited a second, tapping her fingers on the steering wheel before saying, "I know. My family warns me about it all the time."

He touched her shoulder for emphasis. "Then, maybe you should listen to them."

He suddenly realized touching her had been a mistake. With her layered clothing he was far from coming into contact with bare skin, but he could still feel sensuous heat swelling his fingertips.

"I try to listen."

The catch in her voice sent a ripple of desire through him. He shifted in his seat when a thrumming dose of heat ripped through his gut. "Maybe you should try harder, Bailey."

What made Walker so different from any other man? His touch on her shoulder affected her in a way no man's touch had ever affected her before. How did he have the ability to reach her inner being and remind her that she was a woman?

Personal relationships weren't her forte. Most of the guys in these parts were too afraid of her brothers and cousins to even think of crossing the line, so she'd only had one lover. For her it had been one and done, and executed more out of curiosity than anything else. She certainly hadn't been driven by the kind of sexual desire she was feeling with Walker.

There was a spike of heat that always rolled in her stomach whenever she was around him, not to mention the warmth that settled in the area between her legs. Even now, just being in the same vehicle with him was making her breasts tingle. Had his face inched a little closer to hers?

Suggesting they go for a late-night ride might not have been a good idea after all. "I'm not perfect," she finally said softly.

"No one is perfect," he responded huskily.

Bailey drew in a sharp breath when he rubbed a finger across her cheek. She fought back the slow moan that threatened to slip past her lips. His hand on her shoulder had caused internal havoc; his fingers on her face were stirring something to life inside her that she'd never felt before.

She needed to bring an end to this madness. The last thing she wanted was for him to misunderstand the reason she'd brought him here. "I didn't bring you out here for this, Walker," she said. "I don't want you getting the wrong idea."

"Okay, what's the right idea?" he asked, leaning in even closer. "Why did you bring me out here?"

Nervously, she licked her lips. He was still rubbing a finger across her cheek. "To apologize."

"Apology accepted." Then he lowered his head and took possession of her mouth.

Five

Walker deepened the kiss, even while trying to convince himself that he should not be kissing Bailey. No way should his tongue be tangling with hers or hers with his.

But she tasted so damn good. And he didn't want to stop. Truth be told, he'd been anxiously waiting for this minute. He would even admit he'd waited ever since that day at the airport when he'd first thought her lips were a luscious pair. A pair he wanted to taste. Now he was getting his chance.

Her tongue was driving him insane. Her taste was hot, simply addictive. She created a wildness within him, unleashing a sexual beast that wanted to consume every bone-melting inch of her. When had he kissed any woman so thoroughly, with such unapologetic rawness?

He tangled his fingers in her hair, holding her mouth captive as his mouth and tongue sucked, licked and teased every delicious inch of her mouth. This kiss was so incredibly pleasurable his testicles ached. If he didn't end things now, this kiss could very well penetrate his very soul.

He reluctantly broke off the kiss, but made sure his mouth didn't stray far. He could feel the sweet, moist heat of her breath on his lips and he liked it. He liked it so much that he gave in to temptation and used his tongue to trace a path along her lips. Moments later that same tongue tracked a line down her neck and collarbone before returning to her mouth.

She slowly opened her eyes and looked at him. He knew he shouldn't be thinking it, but at that moment he wished the truck had a backseat. All the things he would do to her filled his mind.

"That was some acceptance," she whispered hotly against his lips.

He leaned forward and nibbled around her chin. "Acceptance of what?"

"My apology. Maybe I should apologize more often."

He chuckled lightly, leaning back to meet her gaze. "Do you often do or say things that require an apology?"

"So I'm told. I'm known to put my foot in my mouth more often than not. But do you know what?"

"What?"

"I definitely like your tongue in my mouth a lot better, Walker."

Walker drew in a ragged breath. He was learning there was no telling what would come out of that luscious mouth of hers. "No problem. That can be arranged."

He leaned in and kissed her again; this time was more intense than the last. He figured he needed the memory of this kiss to take back to Kodiak for those long cold nights, when he would sit in front of the fireplace alone and nurse a bottle of beer.

She was shivering in his arms and he knew it had nothing to do with the temperature. She was returning his kiss in a way that ignited every cell in his body, and tasted just as incredibly sexy as she looked. Never had he sampled a woman whose flavor fired his blood to a degree where he actually felt heat rushing through his veins.

He could do a number on her mouth forever, and would have attempted to do so if he hadn't felt her fingers fumbling with the buttons on his shirt. He needed to end this now or else he would be a goner. There was only so much he could take when it came to Bailey.

Walker broke off the kiss, resting his forehead against hers. The needs filtering through him were as raw as raw could get. Primitive. It had been years since a woman had filled him with such need. He was like a starving man who was only hungry for her.

"I didn't bring you out here for this, Walker."

Her words had come out choppy but he understood them. "You said that already." He kept his forehead plastered to hers. There was something so alluring about having his mouth this close to hers. At any time he could use his tongue to swipe a taste of her.

"I'm saying it again. I only wanted to park and talk."

He chuckled against her lips. "That's all?"

Now it was her turn to chuckle. "You are so typically male. Ready to get laid, any time or any place."

"Um, not really. I have very discriminating taste. And speaking of taste," he said, leaning back slightly so he could look into her eyes, "I definitely like yours."

Bailey nervously licked her lips. What was a woman supposed to say to a line like that? In all honestly, there was nothing she could say, especially while gazing into the depths of Walker's dark eyes. He held her gaze hostage and there was nothing she could do about it. Mainly because there was nothing she wanted to do about it. His eyes had her mesmerized, drawing her under his spell.

The same thing had happened earlier when she'd watched his two movies back-to-back. What Chloe had said was true. His performances in both roles had been award-worthy material. Sitting there, watching him on her television screen, was like watching a totally different person. She could see how he'd become a heartthrob in a short period of time. His sexiness had been evident in his clothes, his voice and the roles he'd chosen. And those lovemaking scenes had blazed off the charts. They'd left her wishing she had been the woman in those scenes with him. And tonight, as unbelievable as it seemed, she had lived her own memorable scene with him.

She had to remember the reason she had brought him here. Apologizing for last night was only part of it. "There's something else I need to talk to you about, Walker."

He tipped his head back. "Is there?"

"Yes."

"Can I kiss you again first?" he asked, rubbing his thumb over her bottom lip.

Bailey knew she should say no. Another kiss from him was the last thing she needed. She feared it would detonate her brain. But her brain was halfway gone already, just from the sensuality she heard in his voice. His thumb gently stroking her lip stirred a need that primed her for something she couldn't define but wanted anyway.

He was staring at her, waiting for an answer. She could feel the effects of his spellbinding gaze all over her body. Suddenly she felt bold, empowered, filled with a burning need. Instead of answering him, she pushed in the center console, converting the truck from bucket seats to bench seats. Easing closer to him, she wrapped her arms around his neck and tilted her mouth up to his. "Yes, Walker. You can kiss me again."

And as if that was all he needed to hear, he swooped down and sucked her tongue into his mouth. Bailey couldn't help but moan. He was consuming her. She sensed a degree of hunger within him she hadn't recognized in the other kisses. It was as if he was laying claim to her mouth, branding it in a way no other man had or ever would, and all while his knuckles softly stroked her jaw.

She kissed him back with the same greediness. No matter what costar she'd watched him with earlier, he was with her now. This was real, no acting involved. The only director they were following was their own desire, which seemed to be overtaking them.

Walker's hand reached under her sweater to caress her stomach, and she moaned at the contact. The feel of his fingers on her bare flesh made her shiver, and when he continued to softly rub her skin she closed her eyes as awareness spiked fully into her blood.

The moment he released her mouth, she leaned closer and used her tongue to lick the corners of his lips. His hand inched upward, stroking her ribs, tracing the contours of her bones until he reached her breasts. She drew in a deep breath when his fingertips drew circles on the lace bra covering her nipples. The twin buds hardened and sent a signal to the juncture of her thighs. When he pushed her sweater out of the way, her body automatically arched toward him.

As if he knew what she wanted, what she needed, he undid the front clasp of her bra. As soon as her breasts sprang free, he lowered his mouth to them. Her nipples were hard and ready for him and he devoured them with a greediness that had her moaning deep in her throat.

When she felt the truck's leather touch her back, she realized he had lowered her onto her back. She ran her hands over his shirt and began undoing the buttons, needing to touch his bare skin like he was touching hers. Moments later, her fingers speared into the hair covering his chest.

She heard him growl her name seconds before he captured her wrists, holding her captive while his tongue swirled languorously over her stomach. Her skin sizzled everywhere his mouth touched. And when his mouth reached her navel, he laved it with his tongue. Her stomach muscles flexed beneath his mouth.

Walker was convinced Bailey's body was calling out to him. He was determined to answer the call. She tasted wonderful and when she rocked her body beneath his mouth he couldn't help but groan. His control was eroding. He'd thought all he wanted was a kiss to remember, but he discovered he wanted something more. He wanted her. All of her. He wanted to explode in the heat she was generating. But first, he wanted to fill her with the rapturous satisfaction she needed.

Raising his head, he met her gaze. The fire in her eyes almost burned him. "Lift up your hips, Bailey," he whispered.

When she did as he requested, he unsnapped her jeans and worked the denim down past her thighs. He then grazed his fingers against the scrap of lace covering her femininity. He inhaled deeply, drawing her luscious scent through his nostrils. His heart pounded hard in his chest and every cell in his body needed to please her. To give her a reason to remember him. Why that was important, he wasn't sure. All he knew was that it was.

His erection jerked greedily in anticipation of her feminine taste. When he lowered his head and eased his tongue inside her, he forced himself not to climax just from the delicious flavor of her. She pushed against his shoulders and then, seconds later, gripped him hard, holding his mouth right there as she moaned his name. He delved deep inside, stroking her, lapping up her taste with every inch of his tongue.

She lifted her hips to his mouth and he gripped her thighs tightly, devouring her in a way he'd dreamed of doing every night since he'd met her. Her scent and her taste filled him with emotions and sensations he hadn't felt in years.

He felt her body jerk beneath his mouth in an explosive orgasm. She screamed his name, but he kept his mouth crushed to her, sucking harder and hoping this was one intimate kiss she would never, ever forget.

Moments later, after he felt her body go still, except for the shuddering of her breath, he slowly withdrew his tongue—but not before brushing his lips over her womanly mound. Marking. Branding. Imprinting.

"Walker..."

"Yes, baby. I'm here." He eased over her body and kissed her.

Bailey's breath caught in her throat. When Walker finally released her mouth, she could only lie there enmeshed in a web of sensations that had left her weak but totally fulfilled. Never in her life had she experienced anything like what Walker had done. How he had made her feel. The pleasure had been so sharp she might never recover. He had taken her to rapturous heights she hadn't known existed between a man and a woman.

"I think we better go," Walker said softly as he rezipped her jeans, placing a kiss on her stomach. When she felt the tip of his tongue around her belly button, she whispered his name.

He took his time refastening her bra, cupping her breasts and licking her nipples before doing so. Then he pulled her sweater down before helping her into a sitting position. She was tempted to resist. She wanted to lie there while memories washed over her.

"Your breasts are beautiful, you know, Bailey."

She shook her head. No, she didn't know. No other man had ever complimented her breasts. But then, no other man would have had a reason to do so. She drew in a deep breath, rested her head against the seat and closed her eyes. Had she actually experienced an orgasm from a man going down on her? In a parked truck?

"The lake is beautiful tonight."

How could he talk about how beautiful the lake was after driving her into a sexual frenzy and blowing her mind? And just think, he hadn't even made love to her. What he'd given her was an appetizer. She could only imagine what the full course meal would be like.

She slowly opened her eyes and followed his gaze through the windshield to the lake. She knew he was giving her time to pull herself together, clear her head, finish straightening up her clothes. She took another deep breath. In her mind she could still feel his mouth on her breasts and between her thighs. It took her a while to respond to what he'd said. "Yes, it's beautiful. I love coming here. Day or night. Whenever I need to think."

"I can see this being a good thinking spot."

She decided not to add that he'd just proved it was a good making-out spot, as well. She glanced over at him and saw the buttons of his shirt were still undone, reminding her of when her tongue had licked his skin. Her blood seared at the memory.

"What we did tonight was wrong, Bailey. But I don't regret it."

She didn't regret it, either. The only thing she regretted was not taking things further. They were adults, not kids. Consenting adults. And if they had enjoyed it, then what was the problem? "And why was it wrong?"

"Because you deserve more than a meaningless affair and that's all I can offer you."

She didn't recall asking for more. "What makes you think I want any more than that, Walker? I'm not into serious relationships, either. They can get messy."

He lifted a brow. "How so?"

"Men have a tendency to get possessive, territorial. Act crazy sometimes. Trust me, I know. I grew up with twelve of them. That's why I have my rules."

"Bailey's Rules, right?"

"Yep. Those are the ones."

"So if you don't do affairs, what do you do? I assume you date."

"When it suits me." No need to tell him she'd never had a steady boyfriend. "I assume you date, too."

"Yes, when it suits me," he said, repeating her words.

"So we understand each other," she said, wondering if they really did.

"Yes, I guess you can say that," he said, buttoning his shirt. "And now is as good a time as any to mention that I've decided to return to Kodiak right after the wedding on Saturday instead of on Monday as planned."

Her jaw dropped in surprise. "You're leaving Saturday?"

"Yes."

"Why?"

He looked over at her. "There's no need to stay here any longer than that. What I have to tell the Outlaws won't change. Your family is good people, and it will be Garth and his brothers' loss if they listen to Bart and decide not to meet all of you."

She didn't say anything while she considered her plans for him to be interviewed by one of her writers. "I need you to stay until Monday...at least."

He glanced over at her with keen, probing eyes. "Why do you need me to stay until Monday?"

Something cautioned her to choose her words carefully. "Remember earlier, I told you there was something else I needed to discuss with you?"

He nodded. "Yes, I remember."

"Well, it was about a favor I need to ask."

"What kind of favor?"

She nervously nibbled at her bottom lip. "Today I found out that you used to be an actor. Ty Reklaw."

He didn't say anything for a minute. "So what of it? And what does that have to do with me staying until Monday?"

She heard a tinge of annoyance in his voice and had a feeling he didn't like being reminded of his past. "I understand you were at the peak of your acting career when you left Hollywood to return to Alaska. I was sorry to hear about you losing your family. Must have been a difficult time for you."

She paused and when he didn't say anything, she pressed on. "It's been almost ten years and you're still alone, living on your island. It just so happens that *Simply Irresistible* will be doing an article about men who are loners and I would love to make you our feature story."

He still didn't say anything. He merely stared at her. She swallowed deeply, hesitating only a second before asking, "So will you do it? Will you let me schedule an interview for you with one of my writers to be our feature story?"

It was then, there in the moonlight, that she saw the stiffening of his jaw and the rage smoldering in his gaze. "No. And you have a lot of damn nerve. Is that what this little truck ride was about, Bailey? How far did you intend to go to get me to say yes?"

Her gaze narrowed. "What are you asking? Are you insinuating I used my body to get my way?"

"Why not? I've been approached in the past by reporters who will do just about anything for a story."

"Well, I'm not one of them. The main reason I asked you here was to apologize for my behavior last night. Then I wanted to ask a favor of you."

"And why do you think I would want to be interviewed?

I left Hollywood for a reason and I've never looked back. Why would I want to relive those years?"

"You have it all wrong. The article we plan to publish will have nothing to do with your time in Hollywood. You're a loner and we want to find out why some men prefer that kind of life."

"Have you ever considered the fact that not everyone needs to constantly be around people? It's not as if I'm some damn recluse. I have friends. Real friends. Friends who know how to respect my privacy when I need them to. And they are the ones whose company I seek."

"Yes, however—"

"But you wouldn't understand that. You're dependent on your family for your livelihood, your happiness and your very reason for breathing. That's probably why you've made it one of your rules never to stray too far away from them."

His words fired her up. "And is there anything wrong with that?"

"Not if that's how you choose to live. Which is nobody's business. Just like how I choose to live is nobody's business, either. What makes you think I want to broadcast how I chose to live after losing two of the most important people in my life?"

He wasn't letting her get a word in. "If you just let me finish, I can explain wh—"

"There's nothing to explain. You just got this promotion to features editor and you need a story. Sorry, I refuse to accommodate you. Go find your story someplace else."

An hour or so later, Walker was back in his guest room and still finding it hard to accept the ease with which Bailey had asked that favor of him. Did she not realize the magnitude of the favor she'd asked or did she not care? Was she so into her family that she had no understanding or concept that some people preferred solitude? That not everyone wanted a crowd?

He could only shake his head, since he doubted he could get any angrier than he was at that minute. And he had just warned himself not to let her or any woman who'd shown the same persuasive powers Kalyn had possessed to get close to him. Yet he'd fallen under Bailey's spell after that first kiss. After the second, he'd been a goner.

Even now, memories of those kisses were embedded into the core of his soul. The mere idea of another woman getting that much under his skin stopped him cold with a helplessness he felt in every bone of his body.

He let out a slow, controlled breath. In less than a week he'd allowed Bailey to penetrate an area of his mind he'd thought dead forever. And earlier tonight when he'd reached across the seat and dragged her body against his, it hadn't mattered that they were both fully clothed. Just the idea of her being in his arms had brought out his primitive animal instincts. He'd wanted to mate with her. How he'd found the strength to deny what they'd both wanted was beyond his ability to comprehend, but he had. And for that he was grateful. There was no telling how far she would have gone to get her story. She might have had him eating out of her hands while he spilled his guts.

A part of him wanted to think she was just a woman, easy to forget. But he knew she wasn't just any woman. She wasn't the only person with rules, and somehow Bailey had breached all the rules he'd put in place. At the top of his list was not letting another woman get to him.

Whether it was her making him smile or her making him frown, or her filling him with the degree of anger like he was feeling now—she made him feel too much.

He heard the sound of doors opening and closing downstairs and figured the card game had run its course. Pretty much like he'd run his.

It would be to his advantage to remain true to what he knew. Bailey called it being a loner, but he saw it as surviving.

Bailey glanced at her watch as she got out of her truck once she'd reached Ramsey's Web. Most of her day had been filled with meetings, getting to know her new staff as they got to know her management style. It was important for them to know they were a team.

However, no matter how busy she'd stayed today, thoughts of Walker had filled her mind. He was furious with her, angrier than he'd been two nights ago. Was his anger justified? Had she crossed the line in asking him to do that piece for the magazine?

She was still upset about his insinuation that she would go as far as to use her body to get what she wanted. She didn't play those kinds of games, and for him to assume she did didn't sit well with her. So the way she saw it, they'd both been out of line. They'd both said things they probably regretted today. But she had to remember that Walker was a guest of her family, and the last thing she wanted to be was guilty of offending him. Dillon had placed a lot of confidence in her, and her family would never forgive her if she had offended Walker.

She needed to talk to someone about it before she saw Walker today, and the two people she could always go to for advice were Dillon and Ramsey. There was a chance she would run into Walker at Dillon's place, so she thought it best to seek out Ramsey and ask how she could fix things with Walker before the situation got too out of hand.

She found her eldest brother in his six-car garage with his head stuck under the hood of his Jeep. She loved Ramsey's Web and during her brother's before-Chloe days, she'd spent time here getting deliberately underfoot, knowing he wouldn't have it any other way. The two years when Ramsey had lived in Australia had been hard for her.

The sound of her footsteps must have alerted him to her presence. He lifted his head and smiled at her. "Bay? How are things going?"

"Fine. I would give you a hug but I don't want grease all over me. Why are you changing your oil instead of letting JoJo do it?"

Ramsey chuckled as he wiped his hands. "Because there are some things I'd rather do myself, especially to this baby here. She's been with me since the beginning."

Bailey nodded. She knew the Jeep had been Ramsey's first car and the last gift he'd gotten from their parents. It had been a birthday gift while he'd been in college. "You still keep it looking good."

"Always." He leaned back against the Jeep and studied her curiously. "So what's going on with you, Bailey Joleen Westmoreland?"

This was her eldest brother and he'd always had the ability to read her when others couldn't. "It's Walker."

He lifted a brow. "What about Walker?"

She glanced down at her pointed-toe boots a second before meeting Ramsey's gaze. "I think I might have offended him."

Ramsey crossed his arms over his chest, and she could tell from his expression that he didn't like the sound of that. "How?"

"It's a long story."

"Start from the beginning. I have time."

So she did, not rushing through most of the story and deliberately leaving out some parts. Such as how she'd found Walker utterly attractive from the first, how they'd both tried to ignore the sexual chemistry between them and how they'd made out in her truck last night.

"Well, there you have it, Ram. I apologized to him last

night about my wrong assumptions about his feelings on marriage, but I made him mad again when I asked him to do the interview."

Ramsey shook his head. "Let me get this straight. You found out he used to be a movie star who left Hollywood after the deaths of his wife and child, yet you wanted to interview him about being a loner since that time?"

Ramsey sounded as if he couldn't believe she'd done such a thing. "But that wasn't going to be the angle to the story," she argued. "*Simply Irresistible* isn't a tabloid. I'm not looking for details of his life in Hollywood. Women are curious about men who hang back from the crowd. Not everyone is interested in a life-of-the-party type of male. Women see loners as mysterious and want to know more about them. I thought Walker would be perfect since he's lived by himself for ten years on that ranch in Alaska. I figured he could shed some light on what it's like to be a loner."

"Think about what you were asking him to do, Bay. You were asking to invade his space, pry into his life and make public what he probably prefers to keep private. I bet if you had run your idea by Chloe or Lucia, they would have talked you out of it. Your plan was kind of insensitive, don't you think?"

With Ramsey presenting it that way she guessed it was. She honestly hadn't thought about it that way. She had seen an opportunity and jumped without thinking. "But I would have made the Hollywood part of his life off-limits. It was the loner aspect I wanted to concentrate on. I tried to explain that to him."

"And how were you planning to separate the two? Our pasts shape us into the people we are today. Look at you. Like him, you suffered a double loss. A quadruple one, to be exact. And look how you reacted. Would you want someone to show up and ask to interview you about that?

How can you define the Bailey you are today without re-membering the old you, and what it took to make you grow from one into the other?"

His question had her thinking.

"And I think you missed the mark on something," he added.

She lifted a brow. "What?"

"Assuming being a loner means being antisocial. You can be a loner and still be close to others. Everybody needs some *me* time. Some people need it more so than others. Case in point, I was a loner before Chloe. Even when I had all of you here with me in Westmoreland Country, I kept to myself. At night, when I came here alone, I didn't need anyone invading my space."

She nodded, realizing something. "But I often invaded it, Ram."

"Yes, you did."

Bailey wondered, for the first time, if he had minded. As if reading her thoughts, he said, "No, Bay. Your im-promptu visits never bothered me. All I want you to see is that not everyone needs a crowd. Some people can be their own company, and it's okay."

That was practically what Walker had said. In fact, he had gone even further by saying she was dependent on a crowd. Namely, her large family.

"Looks as if I need to apologize to Walker again. If I keep it up, he's going to think 'I'm sorry' is my middle name. Guess I'll go find him."

"That's going to be pretty difficult."

Her brow furrowed. "Why?"

"Because Walker isn't here. He's left."

"Left?"

"Yes, left. He's on his way back to Alaska. Zane took him to the airport around noon."

"B-but he had planned to stay for the wedding. He

hadn't met everyone since some of the cousins won't be coming in until tomorrow."

"Couldn't be helped. He claimed something came up on his ranch that he had to take care of."

What Ramsey didn't say, but what she figured he was thinking, was that Walker's departure had nothing to do with his ranch and everything to do with her. "Fine. He left. But I'm going to apologize to him anyway."

"Um, I probably wouldn't ask Dillon for Walker's phone number if I were you, especially not if you tell him the same story you just told me."

Bailey nibbled her bottom lip. How was she going to get out of the mess she'd gotten herself into?

Six

"So tell me again why you cut the trip short."

Walker glared across the kitchen at his best friend, who had made himself at home, sitting at Walker's table and greedily devouring a bowl of cereal.

"Why? I've told you once already. The Westmorelands are legit. I didn't have to prolong the visit. Like I said, no matter what Bart believes, I think you and your brothers should take them seriously. They're good people."

Walker turned to the sink with the pretense of rinsing out his coffee cup. What he'd told Garth about the Westmorelands being good people was true—up to a point. As far as he was concerned, the jury was still out on Bailey.

Bailey.

There was no way Walker could have hung around another day and breathed the same air that she did. He clenched his jaw at the thought that he had allowed her to get under his skin. She was just the type who could get embedded in a man's soul if he was weak enough to let it happen.

On top of everything else, she was as gutsy as the day was long. She'd definitely had a lot of nerve asking him to do that interview. She was used to getting what she wanted, but he wasn't one of her brothers or cousins. He had no reason to give in to her every wish.

"You actually played cards with Thorn Westmoreland?" Garth asked with what sounded like awe.

"Yes," Walker said over his shoulder. "He told us about the bike he's building for some celebrity."

"Really? Did you mention that you used to be an actor and that you know a lot of those folks in Hollywood?"

"No."

"Why not?"

Walker turned around. "I was there to get to know them, not the other way around, Garth. They didn't need to know anything about me other than that I was a friend to the Outlaws who came in good faith to get to know them."

But that hadn't stopped them from finding out about his past anyway. He wasn't sure who all knew, since the only person who'd mentioned anything about his days in Hollywood was Bailey. If the others knew, they'd been considerate enough to respect his privacy. That had been too much to expect of Bailey. All she'd seen was an opportunity to sell magazines.

"I think I'll take your advice and suggest to the others that we pay those Westmorelands a visit. In fact, I'm looking forward to it."

"You won't be disappointed," Walker said, opening the dishwasher to place his cup inside. "How are you going to handle Bart? Do you have any idea why he's so dead set against any of you establishing relationships with your new cousins?"

"No, but it doesn't matter. He'll have to get over it."

Garth glanced at his watch. "I hate to run but I have a meeting back in Fairbanks in three hours. That will give Regan just enough time to fly me out of here and get me back to the office."

Regan Fairchild had been Garth's personal pilot for the past two years. She'd taken her father's place as the corporate pilot for the Outlaws after he retired. "I'll see you out."

When they passed through the living room, Garth glanced over at Walker. "When you want to tell me the real reason you left Denver early, let me know. Don't forget I can read you like a book, Walker."

Walker didn't want to hear that. "Don't waste your time. Go read someone else."

They had almost made it across the room when Walker's doorbell sounded. "That's probably Macon. He's supposed to stop by today and check out that tractor he wants to buy from me."

They had reached the door and, without checking to see who was on the other side, Walker opened it. Shocked, his mouth dropped open as his gaze raked over the woman standing there.

"Hello, Walker."

He recovered, although not as quickly as he would have liked. "Bailey! What the hell are you doing here?"

Instead of answering, her gaze shifted to the man standing by his side. "Hey, you look like Riley," she said, as her face broke into a smile.

It was a smile that Garth returned. "And you look like Charm."

She chuckled. "No, Charm looks like me. I understand I'm older."

"Excuse me for breaking up this little chitchat, but what are you doing here, Bailey?" Walker asked in an annoyed tone.

"Evidently she came here to see you, and on that note,

I am out of here. I need to make that meeting," Garth said, slipping out the door. He looked over his shoulder at Walker with an expression that clearly said, *You have a lot of explaining to do.*

To Bailey, Garth said, "Welcome to Hemlock Row. I'll let the family know you're here. Hopefully Walker will fly you into Fairbanks."

"Don't hold your breath for that to happen," Walker said. He doubted Garth heard as he quickly darted to his parked car. His best friend had a lot of damn nerve. How dare he welcome anyone to Walker's home?

Walker turned his attention back to Bailey, trying to ignore the flutter in his stomach at seeing just how beautiful she looked. Nor did he want to concentrate on her scent, which had filled his nostrils the moment he'd opened the door.

Walker crossed his arms over his chest. "I've asked you twice already and you've yet to answer," he said in a harsh tone. "What are you doing here?"

Bailey blew out a chilled breath, wrapped her arms around herself and tried not to shiver. "Could you invite me inside first? It's cold out here."

He hesitated, as if he were actually considering doing just the opposite, and then he stepped back. She hurriedly came inside and closed the door behind her. She had dressed in layers, double the amount she would have used in Denver, yet she still felt chilled to the bone.

"You might as well come and stand in front of the fireplace to warm up."

"Thanks," she said, surprised he'd made the offer. After sliding the carry-on bag from her shoulders, she peeled off her coat, then her jacket and gloves.

Instead of renting a car, she had opted for a cab service, even though the ride from the airstrip had cost her a pretty penny. But she hadn't cared. She'd been cold, exhausted and determined to get to Walker's place before nightfall.

The cabbie had been chatty, explaining that Walker seldom got visitors and trying to coax her into telling him why she was there. She'd let him talk, and when he'd figured out she wasn't providing any information, he'd finally lapsed into silence. But only for a little while. Then he'd pointed out a number of evergreen trees and told her they were mountain hemlocks, a tree common to Alaska. He'd told her about the snowstorm headed their way and said she'd made it to the island just in time or she would have been caught in it. Sounded to her as if she would get caught in it anyway since her return flight was forty-eight hours from now. The man had been born and raised on the island and had a lot of history to share.

When the cabbie had driven up to the marker for Hemlock Row, the beautiful two-story ranch house that sat on Walker's property made her breath catch. It was like looking at a gigantic postcard. It had massive windows, multiple stone chimneys and a wraparound porch. It sat on the Shelikof Strait, which served as a backdrop that was simply beautiful, even if it was out in the middle of nowhere and surrounded by snow. The only other house they'd passed had to be at least ten to fifteen miles away.

Walker's home was not as large as Dillon's, but like Dillon's, it had a rustic feel, as if it belonged just where it sat.

"Drink this," Walker said, handing her a mug filled with hot liquid. She hadn't realized he'd left her alone. She'd been busy looking around at the furniture, which seemed warm and welcoming.

"Thanks." She took a sip of what tasted like a mixture of coffee, hot chocolate and a drop of tea. It tasted delicious. As delicious as Walker looked standing directly in front of her, barefoot, with an open-collar sweater and jeans riding low on his hips. What man looked this mouthwatering so early in the day? Had it really been a week since she'd seen him last? A week when she'd thought about him every day, determined to make this trip to Kodiak Island, Alaska, to personally deliver the apology she needed to make.

"Okay, now that you've warmed up, how about telling me what you're doing here."

She lowered the cup and met his gaze. After telling Lucia and Chloe what she'd done and what she planned to do, they had warned her that Walker probably wouldn't be happy to see her. She could tell from the look on his face that they'd been right. "I came to see you. I owe you an apology for what I said. What I suggested doing with that piece for the magazine."

He frowned. "Why are you apologizing? Doing something so inconsiderate and uncaring seems to be so like you."

His words hurt but she couldn't get mad. That was unfortunately the way she'd presented herself since meeting him. "That goes to show how wrong you are about me and how wrong I was for giving you reason to think that way."

"Whatever. You shouldn't have bothered. I don't think there's anything you can do or say to change my opinion of you."

That angered her. "I never realized you were so judgmental."

"I'm as judgmental as you are."

She wondered if all this bitterness and anger were necessary. Possibly, but at the moment she was too exhausted to deal with it. What should have been a fifteen-hour flight had become a twenty-two-hour flight when the delay of one connection had caused her to miss another. On top of everything else, due to the flight chaos, her luggage was heaven knew where. The airline assured her it would be found and delivered to her within twenty-four hours. She hoped that was true because she planned to fly out again in two days.

"Look, Walker. My intentions were good, and regardless of what you think of me I did come here to personally apologize."

"Fine. You've apologized. Now you can leave.'

"Leave? I just got here! Where am I to go?"

He frowned. "How did you get here?"

"I caught a taxi from the airport."

A dark brow lowered beneath a bunched forehead. "Then, call them to come pick you up."

He couldn't be serious. "And go where? My return flight back to Denver isn't for forty-eight hours."

His frown deepened. "Then, I suggest you stay with your cousins in Fairbanks. You've met Garth. He will introduce you to the others."

Her spine stiffened. "Why can't I wait it out here?"

He glared at her. "Because you aren't welcome here, Bailey."

Walker flinched at the harshness of his own words. He regretted saying them the moment they left his lips. He could tell by the look on her face that they'd hurt her. He then remembered how kind her family had been to him, a virtual stranger, and he knew that no matter how he felt about her, she didn't deserve what he'd just said. But then, what had given her the right to come here uninvited?

He watched as she placed the cup on the table and slid back into her jacket. Then she reached for her coat.

"What the hell do you think you're doing?" he asked, noticing how the loud sound of his voice seemed to blast off the walls.

She lifted her chin as she buttoned up her coat. "What does it look like I'm doing? Leaving. You've made it clear you don't want me here, and one thing I don't do is stay where I'm not wanted."

He wanted to chuckle at that. Hadn't her cousins and brothers told him, jokingly, how she used to impose herself on them? Sometimes she'd even done so purposely, to rattle any of their girlfriends she hadn't liked. "Forget what I said. I was mad."

When her coat was buttoned practically to her neck, she glared at him. "And you're still mad. I didn't come all the way here for verbal abuse, Walker. I came to apologize."

"Apology accepted." The memory of what had followed the last time he'd said those words slammed into his mind. He'd kissed her, feasting on her mouth like a hungry man who'd been denied food for years.

He could tell from the look in her eyes that she was remembering, as well. He figured that was the reason she broke eye contact with him to look at the flames blazing in the fireplace. Too late—the wood burning wasn't the only thing crackling in the room. He could feel that stirring of sensual magnetism that always seemed to surround them. It was radiating more heat than the fireplace.

"Now that I think about it, staying here probably isn't a good idea," she said, glancing back at him.

He released a deep breath and leaned back on his heels. She was right. It wasn't a good idea, but it was too late to think about that now. "A storm's headed this way so it doesn't matter if you don't think it's a good idea."

"It matters to me if you don't want me here," she snapped.

He rubbed his hand down his face. "Look, Bailey. I think we can tolerate each other for the next forty-eight hours. Besides, this place is so big I doubt if I'll even see you during that time." To be on the safe side, he would put her in one of the guest rooms on the south wing. That part of the house hadn't been occupied in over fifteen years.

"Where's your luggage?" he asked. The quicker he could get her settled in, the quicker he could ignore her presence.

"The airline lost it, although they say it has just been misplaced. They assured me they will deliver it here within twenty-four hours."

That probably wasn't going to happen, he thought, but figured there was no reason to tell her that. "Just in case they're delayed, I have a couple of T-shirts you can borrow to sleep in."

"Thanks."

"If you're hungry I can fix you something. I hadn't planned on preparing dinner till later, but there are some leftovers I can warm up."

"No, thanks. I'm not hungry. But I would appreciate if I could wash up and lie down for a bit. The flight from Anchorage was sort of choppy."

"Usually it is, unfortunately. I'll show you up to the room you'll be using. Just follow me."

Seven

The sound of a door slamming somewhere in the house jarred Bailey awake and had her scrambling to sit up in bed and try to remember where she was. It all came tumbling back to her. Kodiak Island, Alaska. Walker's ranch.

She settled back down in bed, remembering the decision she had made to come here. She could finally admit it had been a bad one. Hadn't Walker said she wasn't welcome? But she had been determined to come after deciding a phone-call apology wouldn't do. She needed to tell him in person that she was sorry.

And she would even admit that a part of her had wanted to see him face-to-face. Everyone in the family had been surprised he'd left early, and although no one questioned her about it, she knew they suspected she was to blame. And she had been. So no one had seemed surprised when she announced her plans to travel to Kodiak. However, Dillon had pulled her aside to ask if that was something she really wanted to do. She'd assured him that it was, and told him she owed Walker an apology and wanted to deliver it to him personally.

So here she was, in an area as untamed and rugged as the most remote areas of Westmoreland Country. But there were views she had passed in the cab that had been so beautiful they had almost taken her breath away. Part of her couldn't wait to see the rest of it.

Bailey heard the sound of a door slamming again and glanced over at the clock on the nightstand. Had she slept for four hours?

She suddenly sniffed the air. Something smelled good, downright delicious. Walker had been cooking. She hoped he hadn't gone to any trouble just for her. When her stomach growled she knew she needed to get out of bed and go downstairs.

She recalled Walker leading her up to this room and the two flights of stairs they'd taken to get here. The moment she'd followed him inside she'd felt something she hadn't felt in years. Comfort. Somehow this guest room was just as warm and welcoming as the living room had been.

It might have been the sturdy-looking furniture made of dark oak. Or the huge bed that had felt as good as it looked. She couldn't wait to sleep in it tonight. Really sleep in it. Beneath the covers and not on top like she'd done for her nap. Getting out of bed, she headed for the bathroom, glad she at least had her carry-on containing her makeup and toiletries.

A few minutes later, feeling refreshed and less exhausted, she left the guest room to head downstairs. She hoped Walker was in a better mood than he'd been in earlier.

Walker checked the timer on the stove before lifting the lid to stir the stew. He'd cooked more than the usual amount since he had a houseguest. Bailey had been asleep for at least four hours and even so, her presence was disrupting his normal routine. He would have driven around his land by now, checking on the herds and making sure everything was ready for the impending snowstorm. He'd talked to Willie, his ranch foreman, who had assured him everything had been taken care of.

That brought his thoughts back to Bailey, and he uttered an expletive under his breath. He'd figured out the real reason, the only one that made sense, as to why she was here, using an apology as an excuse. She probably thought she could make him change his mind about doing the interview, but she didn't know how wrong she was.

As far as he was concerned, she'd wasted her time coming here. Although he had to admit it had been one hell of a gutsy move. As gutsy as it was crazy. He'd warned her the first day they'd met that winters in Alaska were a lot worse than the coldest day in Denver. Evidently she hadn't believed him and now would find out the truth for herself. She had arrived nearly frozen.

But nearly frozen or not, that didn't stop the male in him from remembering how good she'd looked standing on his porch. Or how she'd looked standing by his fireplace after she'd removed layer after layer of clothing.

He had awakened this morning pretty much prepared for anything. He figured it was only a matter of time before Garth showed up. And a snowstorm blowing in was the norm. What he hadn't counted on was Bailey showing up out of Alaska's cold blue sky. When he'd left Denver, he had assumed their paths wouldn't cross again. There was no reason why they should. Even if the Outlaws kindled a relationship with the Westmorelands, that wouldn't necessarily mean anything to *him*, because he lived here on the island and seldom flew to Fairbanks.

"Sorry I overslept."

He turned around and then wished he hadn't. She was

still wearing the clothes she'd had on earlier, since she didn't have any others, but his gaze moved beyond that. From what he could tell, she wasn't wearing any makeup and she had changed her hairstyle. It no longer hung around her shoulders but was pulled back in a ponytail. The style made her features look younger, delicate and sexy enough to make his lower body throb.

"No problem," he said, turning his attention back to the stove.

He'd seen enough of her. Too much for his well-being. Having her standing in the middle of his kitchen, a place he'd never figured she would be, was sending crazy thoughts through his head. Like how good she looked in that particular spot. A spot where Kalyn had never stood. In fact, his wife had refused to come to Kodiak. She hadn't wanted to visit the place where he was born. Had referred to it as untamed wilderness that lacked civilization. She hadn't wanted to visit such a remote area, much less live there. She was a California girl through and through. She'd lived for the beaches, the orange groves and Hollywood. Anything else just didn't compute with her.

"What are you cooking? Smells good."

He inwardly smiled, although he didn't want to. Was that her way of letting him know she was hungry? "Bison stew. My grandmother's recipe," he said over his shoulder.

"No wonder it smells good, then."

Now, aren't you full of compliments, he thought sarcastically, knowing she was probably trying to be nice for a reason. But he wasn't buying it, because he knew her motives. "By the time you wash up I'll have dinner on the table."

"I've washed up and I can help. Thanks to Chloe I'm pretty good in the kitchen. Tell me what you need me to do."

"Why Chloe?"

"In addition to all her other talents, she is a wonderful

cook and often prepares breakfast for Ramsey and his men. Remind me to tell you one day how she and Ramsey met."

He came close to saying that he wouldn't be reminding her of anything, and he didn't need her to do anything, unless she could find her way back to the airport. But he reined in his temper and said, "You can set the table. Everything you need is in that drawer over there." He never ate at a set table but figured it would give her something to do so she wouldn't get underfoot. Not that trying to put distance between them really mattered. Her scent had already downplayed the aroma of the stew.

The ringing of his cell phone on the kitchen counter jarred him out of his thoughts. He moved from the stove to pick it up, recognizing his foreman's ringtone.

"Yes, Willie? What is it?"

"It's Marcus, boss," Willie said in a frantic tone. "A big brown's got him pinned in a shack and nothing we can do will scare him off. We've been firing shots, but we haven't managed a hit."

"Damn. I'm on my way."

Walker turned and quickly moved toward the closet where his parkas hung and his boots were stored. "Got to go," he said quickly. "That was Willie Hines, my foreman. A brown bear has one of my men holed up in a shack and I need to get there fast."

"May I go?"

He glanced over his shoulder to tell her no. Then he changed his mind. It probably had something to do with that pleading look on her face. "Yes, but stay out of the way. Grab your coat, hat and scarf. And be quick. My men are waiting."

She moved swiftly and by the time he'd put on his boots she was back. He grabbed one of the rifles off the rack. When she reached up and grabbed a rifle off the rack as well, he stared at her. "What do you think you're doing?"

"I'm not a bad shot. Maybe I can help."

He doubted she could and just hoped she stayed out of the way, but he didn't have time to argue. "Fine, let's go."

"I thought bears normally hibernated in the winter," Bailey said, hanging on in the Jeep. Walker was driving like a madman and the seat belt was barely holding her in place. On top of that, her thick wool coat was nothing against the bone-chilling wind and the icy slivers of snow that had begun to fall.

"It's not officially winter yet. Besides, this particular brown is probably the same one who's been causing problems for the past year. Nothing he does is normal. There's been a bounty on his head for a while now."

Bailey nodded. Although bears were known to reside in the Rockies, they were seldom seen. She'd known of only one incident of a bear in Westmoreland Country. Dillon had called the authorities, who had captured the bear and set him free elsewhere. She then remembered what Walker had told her the first day they'd met. There were more bears than people living on Kodiak Island.

The Jeep came to a sudden stop in front of three men she figured worked for Walker. He was out of the truck in a flash and before she could unbuckle her seat belt, he snapped out an order. "Stay put, Bailey."

She grudgingly did as she was told and watched him race toward the men. They pointed at the scene taking place a hundred or so feet ahead of them. The creature wasn't what she'd expected of a brown bear. He was a huge grizzly tearing away at a small, dilapidated shack, pawing through timber, lumber and planks trying to get to the man trapped inside. Unless someone did something, it wouldn't take long for the bear to succeed. And if anyone tried shooting the bear now, they would place the man inside the shack at risk.

She didn't have to hear what Walker and his men were saying to know they were devising a plan to pull the bear's attention away from the shack. And it didn't take long to figure out that Walker had volunteered to be the bait. Putting his own life at risk.

She watched, horrified, as Walker raced forward to get the bear's attention, coming to a stop at what seemed to be just a few feet from the animal. At first it seemed as if nothing could dissuade the bear. A few more loose timbers and he would get his prey. She could hear the man inside screaming in fright, begging for help before it was too late.

Walker then picked up a tree limb and hit the bear. That got the animal's attention. Bailey held her breath when the bear turned and went charging after Walker. The plan was for Walker to lure the bear away from the shack so his men could get a good shot. It seemed the ploy was working until Walker lost his balance and fell to the ground.

Bailey was out of the Jeep in a flash, her rifle in her hand. She stood beside the men and raised her gun to take a shot.

"There's no way you can hit that bear from here, lady," one of the men said.

She ignored his words, knowing Walker would be mauled to death unless she did something. She pulled the trigger mere seconds before the bear reached Walker. The huge animal fell and it seemed the earth shook under the weight.

"Did you see that?"

"She got that grizzly and her rifle doesn't even have a scope on it."

"How can she shoot like that? Where did she come from?"

Ignoring what the three men were saying, she raced over to Walker. "Are you okay?"

"I'm fine. I just banged my leg against that damn rock when I tripped."

Placing her rifle aside, she leaned down to check him

over and saw the red bloodstain on the leg of his jeans. He wasn't fine.

She turned to his men, who were looking at her strangely. "He's injured. I need two of you to lift him and take him to the Jeep. The other one, I need to check on the man in the shack. I think he passed out."

"I said I'm fine, Bailey, and I can walk," Walker insisted.

"Not on that leg." She turned to the men. "Lift him and take him to the truck," she ordered again.

"Don't anyone dare lift me. I said I can walk," Walker snapped at the two men who moved toward him.

"No, you can't walk," she snapped back at him. She then glared at his men, who stood staring, unsure whose orders to follow. "Do it!" she demanded, letting them know she expected her order to be followed regardless of what Walker said.

As if they figured any woman who could shoot that well was a woman whose order should be obeyed, they quickly moved to lift Walker. He spewed expletives, which they all ignored.

"I'll call Doc Witherspoon to come quick," one of the men said after they placed Walker in the Jeep. "And we'll be right behind you to help get him out once you reach the ranch house."

She quickly got in on the driver's side. "Thanks."

She glanced over at Walker, who was now unconscious, and fought to keep her panic at bay. Of all the things she figured she'd have to deal with upon reaching Alaska, killing a grizzly bear hadn't been one of them.

Eight

Walker came awake, then reclosed his eyes when pain shot up his leg. It took him a while before he reopened them. When he did, he noted that he was in his bed and flat on his back. It didn't take him long to recall why. The grizzly.

"Bailey?" he called out softly when he heard a sound from somewhere in the room.

"She's not here, Walker," a deep masculine voice said.

He didn't have to wonder who that voice belonged to. "Doc Witherspoon?"

"Who else? I only get to see you these days when you get banged up."

Walker shook his head, disagreeing. "I never get banged up."

"You did this time. Story has it that bear would have eaten you alive if that little lady hadn't saved you."

The doctor's words suddenly made Walker remember what he'd said earlier. "Bailey's not here? Where is she?"

"She left for the airport."

Airport? Bailey was returning to Denver already? "How long have I been out, Doc?" he asked. A lot of stuff seemed fuzzy in his mind.

"Off and on close to forty-eight hours. Mainly because I gave you enough pain pills to down an elephant. Bailey thought it was best. You needed your rest. On top of all that, you were an unruly patient."

Who cared what Bailey thought when she wasn't there? He then replayed in his mind every detail of that day with the bear. "How's Marcus?"

"I treated him for shock but he's fine now. And since he's a ladies' man, he's had plenty of women parading in and out of his place pretending to be nurses."

Walker nodded, trying to dismiss the miserable feelings flooding through when he thought about Bailey being gone. She'd told him she was returning to Denver within forty-eight hours, so what had he expected? Besides, hadn't he wanted her gone? Hadn't he told her she wasn't welcome? So why was he suddenly feeling so disheartened? Must be the medication messing with his mind.

"You have a nasty cut to the leg, Walker. Went real deep. You lost a lot of blood and I had to put in stitches. You've got several bruised ribs but nothing's broken. If you stay off that leg as much as possible and follow my orders, you'll be as good as new in another week or so. I'll be back to check on you again in a few days."

"Whatever." Walker knew Doc Witherspoon would ignore his surly attitude; after all, he was the same man who'd brought Walker into the world.

Walker closed his eyes. He wasn't sure how long he slept, but when he opened his eyes some time later, it was a feminine scent that awakened him. Being careful not to move his leg, he shifted his head and saw Bailey sitting in the chair by the bed reading a book. He blinked to make sure he wasn't dreaming. It wouldn't be the first time he'd dreamed of her since leaving Denver. But never had he dreamed of her sitting by the bed. In all his dreams she had been in the bed with him.

He blinked again and when she still sat there, he figured it was the real thing. "Doc said you left for the airport."

She glanced over at him and their gazes held. Ripples of awareness flooded through him. Why was her very presence in his room filling every inch of space within it? And why did he want her out of that chair and closer to the bed? Closer to him?

She broke eye contact to brush off a piece of lint from her shirt. "I did leave for the airport. Their twenty-four hours were up and I hadn't gotten my luggage."

"You went to the airport to get your luggage?"

"Yes."

He couldn't explain the relief that raced through him. At the moment he didn't want to explain it. He felt exhausted and was in too much pain to think clearly. "I thought you were on your way back to Denver."

"Sorry to disappoint you."

He drew in a deep breath. She'd misunderstood and was assuming things again. Instead of telling her how wrong she was, he asked, "Well, did you get your luggage?"

"Yes. They'd found it, but were taking their time bringing it here. I guess I wasn't at the top of their priority list."

He bet they wished they hadn't made that mistake. She'd probably given them hell.

"You want something to eat?" she asked him. "There's plenty of bison stew left."

Walker was glad because he was hungry and remembered he'd been cooking the stew when he'd gotten the call about Marcus. "Yes. Thanks."

"I'll be right back."

He watched Bailey get out of the chair and place the

book aside before heading for the door. He couldn't help but appreciate the shape of her backside in sweats. At least his attention to physical details hadn't lessened any. He brought his hand to his jaw and realized he needed to trim his beard.

When Bailey pulled the door shut behind her, Walker closed his eyes and again remembered in full detail everything that had happened down by the shack. The one thing that stuck out in his mind above everything else was the fact that Bailey Westmoreland had saved his life.

"Yes, Walker is fine just bruised and he had to get stiches in his leg," she said to Ramsey on the phone. "I hated killing that bear but it was him or Walker. He was big and a mean one."

"You did what you had to do, Bay. I'm sure Walker appreciated you being there."

"Maybe. Doesn't matter now, though. He's confined to bed and needs help. The doctor wants him to stay off his leg as much as possible. That means I need to tell Chloe and Lucia that I'll need a few more days off. Possibly another week."

"Well, you're in luck because Lucia is here, so I'll let you speak to both her and Chloe. You take care of yourself."

"Thanks, I will. I miss everyone."

"And we miss you. But it's nice to have you gone for a while," he teased.

"Whatever," she said, grinning, knowing he was joking. She was certain every member of her family missed her as much as she missed them.

A short while later she hung up. Chloe and Lucia had understood the situation and told her to take all the time she needed to care for Walker. She appreciated that.

Drawing in a deep breath, she glanced around the kitchen.

Over the past three days she had become pretty familiar with it. She knew where all the cooking equipment was located and had found a recipe book that had once belonged to Walker's grandmother. There was a family photo album located in one of the cabinets. She'd smiled at the pictures of Walker's family, people she figured were his parents and grandparents. But nowhere in the album did she find any of his wedding pictures or photographs of his wife and child.

She looked out the window. It was snowing hard outside and had been for the past two days. She had met all the men who worked on Walker's ranch. They had dropped by and introduced themselves and told her they would take care of everything for their boss. News of her encounter with the bear had spread and a lot of the men stared at her in amazement. She found them to be a nice group of guys. A number of them had worked on the ranch when Walker's father was alive. She could tell from the way they'd inquired about Walker's well-being that they were very fond of him and deeply loyal.

She snorted at the thought of that. They evidently knew a different Walker from the one she'd gotten to know. Due to all the medication the doctor had given him, he slept most of the time, which was good. And he refused to let her assist him to the bathroom or in taking his baths. Doctor Witherspoon had warned him about getting the stitches wet and about staying off his leg as much as possible, so at least he was taking that advice. One of his men had dropped off crutches for him to use, and he was using them, as well.

Snow was coming down even worse now and everything was covered with a white blanket. The men had made sure there was plenty of wood for the fireplace and she had checked and found the freezer and pantry well stocked, so there was nothing for her to do but take things one day at a time while waiting for Walker to get better.

Garth had called for Walker and she'd told him what had happened. He'd left his number and told her to call if she needed anything or if Walker continued to give her trouble. Like she'd told Garth, Walker had pretty much slept for the past three days. When he was awake, other than delivering his meals and making sure he took his medication, she mostly left him alone.

But not today. His bedroom was dark and dreary and although the outside was barely any better, she intended to go into his room and open the curtains. And she intended for him to get out of bed and sit in a chair long enough for her to change the linens.

According to Garth, Walker had a housekeeper, an older woman by the name of Lola Albright, who came in each week, no matter how ugly the weather got outside. She had located Ms. Albright's phone number in the kitchen drawer and called to advise her that she need not come this week. Somehow, but not surprisingly, the woman had already heard what happened. After complimenting Bailey for her skill with a gun, she had thanked Bailey for calling and told her if she needed anything to let her know. Ms. Albright and her husband were Walker's closest neighbors and lived on a farm about ten miles away.

Grabbing the tray with the bowl of chicken noodle soup that she'd cooked earlier, Bailey moved up the stairs to Walker's bedroom. She opened the door and stopped, surprised to see him already out of bed and sitting in the chair.

The first thing she noticed was that he'd shaved. She couldn't stop her gaze from roaming over his face while thinking about just how sexy he looked. He was as gorgeous without facial hair as he was with it. He had changed clothes and was looking like his former self. A part of her was grateful he was sitting up, but then another part of her was annoyed that he hadn't asked for her assistance.

"Lunchtime," she said, moving into the room and put-

ting the tray on a table beside his chair. She wanted to believe he said thanks, although it sounded more like a grunt.
She moved across the room to open the curtains.

"What do you think you're doing?"

Without turning around, she continued opening the curtains. "I thought you might want to look outside."

"I want the curtains closed."

"Sorry, but now they're open." She turned back around
and couldn't help but shiver when she met his stare. His
glare was more like it, but his bad mood didn't bother her.
After five brothers and a slew of male cousins she knew
how to deal with a man who couldn't have his way.

"Glad you're up. I need to change the linens," she said,
moving toward the bed.

"Lola's my housekeeper. She's coming tomorrow and
can do it then."

"I talked to Lola this morning and told her there was
no need for her to come out in this weather. I can handle
things while I'm here."

He didn't say anything but she could tell by his scowl
that he hadn't liked that move. And speaking of moves,
she felt his eyes on her with every move she made while
changing the sheets. She could actually feel his gaze raking across her. When she finished and turned to look at
him, his mouth was set in a hard, tight line.

"You know, if you keep looking all mean and cranky,
Walker, you might grow old looking that way."

His frown deepened. "No matter what you do, I won't
be changing my mind about the interview. So you're wast-
ing your time."

Drawing in a deep, angry breath, she moved across the
room to stand in front of him. She leaned down a little to
make sure her eyes were level with his. "You ungrateful
bastard!"

That was followed by a few more obscenities she hadn't

said since the last time Dillon had washed out her mouth with soap years ago. But Walker's accusations had set her off. "Do you think that's why I'm here? That I only killed that bear, hung around, put up with your crappy attitude just because I want an interview? Well, I've got news for you. I don't want an interview from you. You're no longer a viable candidate. Women are interested in men who are loners but decent, not loners who are angry and couldn't recognize a kind deed if it bit them on the—"

She hadn't expected him to tug on a lock of her hair and capture her mouth. She hadn't expected him to kiss her with a hunger that sent desire raging through her, flooding her with memories of the night they'd parked in her truck at Bailey's Bay.

Convincing herself she was only letting him have his way with her mouth because she didn't want to move and hurt his leg, she found herself returning the kiss, moaning when his tongue began doing all kinds of delicious things to hers.

They were things she had dreamed about, and craved—but only with him. She could admit that at night, in the guest room, in that lonely bed, she had thought of him, although she hadn't wanted to do so. And since all she had were memories, she had recalled how he had licked a slow, wet trail from her mouth to her breasts and then lower.

Her thoughts were snatched back to the present when she felt Walker ease up her skirt and softly skim her inner thighs. His fingers slipped beneath the elastic of her panties before sliding inside her.

She shuddered and his finger moved deeper, pushing her over the edge. She wanted to pull back but couldn't. Instead, she followed his lead and intensified the kiss while his fingers did scandalous things.

Then he released her mouth to whisper against her wet lips, "Come for me again, Bailey."

As if his request was a sensual command her body had to obey, ragged heat rolled in her stomach as her pulse throbbed and her blood roared through her veins. Her body exploded, every nerve ending igniting with an intensity that terrified her. This time was more powerful than the last, and she had no willpower to stop the moan released from her lips. No willpower to stop spreading her thighs wider and arching her mouth closer to once again be taken.

That was when Walker placed his mouth over Bailey's again, kissing her with no restraint. He deepened the kiss, pushing his fingers even farther inside her. He loved the sounds she made when she climaxed; he loved knowing he was the one to make it happen. And he intended to make it happen all over again. Moments later, when she shuddered and groaned into his mouth, he knew he had succeeded.

She grabbed his shoulders, and he didn't flinch when she dug her fingers into his skin. Nor did he flinch when she placed pressure on his tongue. He merely retaliated by sucking harder on hers.

He had been hungry for her taste for days. Each time she had entered his bedroom, he had hated lying flat on his back, not being able to do the one thing he'd wanted to do—kiss her in a way that was as raw as he felt.

Most of the time he'd feigned sleep, but through heavy-lidded eyes he had watched her, studied her and longed for her. He'd known each and every time she had walked around his room, cursing under her breath about his foul mood, using profanity he'd never heard before. He had laid there as his ears burned, pretending to sleep as she called him every nasty name in the book for being so difficult and pigheaded.

He'd also known when she'd calmed down enough to sit quietly in the chair by his bed to read, or softly hum while flipping through one of his wildlife magazines. And he would never forget the day she had worn a sweater and a pair of leggings. She had stretched up to put something away on one of the top shelves in his room and caused his entire body to harden in desire watching her graceful movements. And the outlines of her curves covered by those leggings... His need for her had flowed through him like a potent drug, more intoxicating than the medication Doc Witherspoon had him taking. Knowing she was off-limits, because he had decided it had to be so, had only sharpened his less-than-desirable attitude.

But today had been different. He had awakened with his raging hormones totally out of control. He'd felt better and had wanted to clean himself up, move around and wait for her. He hadn't anticipated kissing her but he was glad he had.

There were multiple layers to Bailey Westmoreland, layers he wanted to unpeel one at a time. The anticipation was almost killing him.

Growling low in his throat, he slowly pulled his mouth away and pulled his fingers from inside her. Then, as she watched, he brought those same fingers to his lips and licked them in slow, greedy movements.

He held her gaze, tempted to take possession of her mouth again. Instead, he whispered, "Thank you for saving my life, Bailey."

He could tell his words of thanks had surprised her. Little did she know she would be in for a few more surprises before she left his ranch to return to Denver.

"And thank you for letting me savor you," he whispered. "To have such a filthy mouth, you have a very delicious taste."

And he meant it. He loved the taste of her on his fingers. Bailey was a woman any man would want to possess. The good. The bad. And the ugly. And for some reason that he didn't understand or could explain, he wanted that man to be him.

With that thought planted firmly in his mind, he leaned close, captured her mouth with his and kissed her once again.

Nine

"What have you gotten yourself into, Bailey?" she asked herself a few days later while standing outside on Walker's front porch.

This was the first time the weather had improved enough for her to be outside. As far as she could see, snow covered everything. It had seemed to her that it hadn't been snowflakes falling for the past several days but ice chips. The force of them had hit the roof, the windowpanes and blanketed the grounds.

Yesterday, Josette told her a bad snowstorm had hit Denver and threatened to close the airport. Bailey had endured Denver's snowstorms all her life, but what she'd experienced over the past few days here in Alaska was far worse. Even though parts of this place reminded her of Denver, looking out at the Strait from her bedroom window meant she saw huge glaciers instead of mountains. And one of the ponds on Walker's property had been a solid block of ice since she'd arrived.

Wrapping her hands around the mug of coffee she held in her hand, she took a sip. Would her question to herself ever be answered? Was there even an answer? All she knew was that she had to leave this place and return home before...

Before what?

Already Walker had turned her normally structured mind topsy-turvy. It had started the day he'd kissed her in his bedroom. Oh, he'd done more than kiss her. He had inserted his fingers inside her and made her come. Just like before. But this time he had tasted her on his fingers, letting her watch. And then he'd kissed her again, letting her taste herself on his lips.

At least when that kiss had ended she'd had the good sense to get out of the room. And she had stayed out until it was time to deliver his dinner. Luckily when she'd entered the room later that day, he had been asleep, so she had left the covered tray of food by his bed. Then Willie had dropped by that evening to visit with Walker and had returned the tray to the kitchen. That had meant she didn't have to go up to his room to get it.

She had checked on him before retiring for the night and he'd been sitting up again, in that same chair. After asking him if there was anything he needed before she went to bed, she had quickly left the room.

That had been three days ago and she'd avoided going into his room since then. She'd only been in to deliver his food. Each time she found him dressed and sitting in that same chair. It was obvious he was improving, so why hadn't she made plans to leave Kodiak Island?

She kept telling herself she wanted to wait until Dr. Witherspoon assured her that Walker could manage on his own. Hopefully, today would be that day. The doctor had arrived an hour ago and was up there with Walker now. It shouldn't be long before Bailey could work her way out of whatever she'd gotten herself into with Walker.

Knowing that if she stayed outside any longer she was liable to turn into a block of ice, she went back inside. She was closing the door behind her as Dr. Witherspoon came down the stairs.

"So how is our patient, Doctor?" she asked the tall, muscular man who reminded her of a lumberjack more than a doctor.

"Walker's fine. The stiches are out and he should be able to maneuver the stairs in a day or so. I'm encouraging him to do so in order to work the stiffness out of his legs."

Bailey nodded as she sat her coffee mug on a side table. "So he's ready to start handling things on his own now?"

"Pretty much, but I still don't want him to overdo it. As you know, Walker has a hard head. I'm glad you're here to make sure he doesn't overexert himself."

Bailey nibbled her bottom lip before saying, "But I can't stay here forever. I have a job back in Denver. Do you have any idea when it will be okay for me to leave?"

"If you have pressing business to attend to back home then you should go now. I'm sure Lola won't mind moving in for a few days until Walker's fully recovered."

Dr. Witherspoon was giving her an out, so why wasn't she taking it? Why was she making herself believe she was needed here?

"Just let me know when you plan to leave so I'll know what to do," the doctor added. "I'm sure you know Walker would prefer to be by himself after you leave, but that's not wise. Personally, I think he needs you."

The doctor didn't know just how wrong he was. Sure, Walker liked kissing her, but that didn't mean he needed her. "I doubt that very seriously. He'll probably be glad to have me gone."

"Um, I don't think so. I've known Walker all his life. I

delivered him into the world and looked forward to delivering his son, but his wife wouldn't hear of it. She wanted their son born in California. She wasn't too fond of this place."

Dr. Witherspoon paused, and a strange look appeared on his face, as if he'd said too much. "Anyway, if you decide to leave before the end of the week, let me know so I can notify Lola."

"I will."

Before reaching the door, the doctor turned. "Oh, yes, I almost forgot. Walker wants to see you."

Bailey lifted a brow. "He does?"

"Yes." The doctor then opened the door and left.

Bailey wondered why Walker would ask to see her. He'd seen her earlier when she'd taken him breakfast. She hadn't been able to decipher his mood, mainly because she hadn't hung around long enough. She'd placed the tray on the table and left. But she had seen that he'd opened the curtains and was sitting in what was evidently his favorite chair.

After taking a deep breath, she moved toward the stairs. She might as well go see what Walker wanted. All things considered, he might be summoning her to ask her to leave.

"Dr. Witherspoon said you wanted to see me."

Walker turned around at the sound of Bailey's voice. She stood in the doorway as if ready to sprint away at a moment's notice. Had his mood been as bad as Doc Witherspoon claimed? If so, she had put up with it when any other woman would not have. "Come in, Bailey, I won't bite."

He wouldn't bite, but he wouldn't mind tasting her mouth again.

She hesitated before entering, looking all around his bedroom before looking back at him. That gave him just enough time to check her out, to appreciate how she looked in her sweats, sweater and jacket. She wore her hair pinned back from her face, which showed off her beautiful bone structure. Although he hadn't stuck around to meet her sister Gemma, he had met Megan. There was a slight resemblance between the two but he thought Bailey had a look all her own. Both were beautiful women but there was a radiance about Bailey that gave him pause whenever he saw her.

"Okay, I'm in," she said, coming to stand in front of him. However, he noted she wasn't all in his face like last time. She was keeping what she figured was a safe distance.

"You're standing up," she observed.

"Is there a reason for me not to be?"

She shrugged. "No. But normally you're sitting down in that chair over there."

He followed her gaze to the chair. "Yes. That chair has special meaning for me."

"It does? Why?"

"It once belonged to my mother. I'm told she used to sit in it and rock me to sleep. I don't recall that, but I do remember coming in here at night and sitting right there on the floor while she sat in that chair and read me a story."

"I heard you tell Dillon you're an only child. Your parents didn't want any more children?"

"They wanted plenty, which is why they built such a huge house. But Mom had difficulties with my birth and Doc Witherspoon advised her not to try again."

"Oh."

A moment of silence settled between them before Bailey said, "You didn't say why you wanted to see me."

No, he hadn't. He stared at her, wishing he wasn't so fascinated with her mouth. "I need to apologize. I haven't been the nicest person the past several days." No need to tell her Doc Witherspoon hadn't spared any punches in telling Walker just what an ass he'd been.

"No, you haven't. You have been somewhat of a grouch, but I've dealt with worse. I have five brothers and a slew of male cousins. I've discovered men can be more difficult than sick babies when they are in pain."

"Regardless, that was no reason to take out my mood on you and I apologize."

She shrugged. "Apology acc—" As if remembering another time those words had set off a kiss between them, she quickly modified her words. "Thank you for apologizing." She turned to leave.

"Wait!"

Bailey turned back around. "Yes?"

"Lunch."

She raised a brow. "What about it?"

"I thought we could eat lunch together."

Bailey eyed Walker speculatively before asking, "Why would you want us to eat lunch together?"

He countered with a question of his own. "Any reason we can't? Although I appreciate you being here, helping out and everything, you're still a guest in my home. Besides, I'm doing better and Doc suggested I try the stairs. I figured we could sit and eat in the kitchen. Frankly, I'm tired of looking at these four walls."

She could see why he would be. "Okay, I'll serve you lunch in the kitchen."

"And you will join me?"

Bailey nibbled her lips. How could she explain that just breathing the same air as him was playing havoc on her nervous system?

Even now, just standing this close to him was messing with her mind. Making her remember things she shouldn't. Like what had happened the last time she'd stayed this long in this bedroom. And he wanted them to share lunch? What would they talk about? One thing was for certain— she would let him lead the conversation. She would not give him any reason to think she was interviewing him undercover. He'd already accused her of having under-handed motives.

When she'd walked into this room, she hadn't counted on him standing in the middle of it. She'd been fully aware of his presence the moment she'd opened the door. He was dressed in a pair of well-worn jeans and a flannel shirt that showed what an impressive body he had. If he'd lost any weight she couldn't tell. He still had a solid chest, broad shoulders and taut thighs. She'd been too taken with all that masculine power to do anything but stand and stare.

Without the beard his jaw looked stronger and his mouth—which should be outlawed—was way too sexy to be real.

Bailey couldn't stop herself from wondering why he wanted to share lunch with her. But then, she didn't want to spend time analyzing his reason. So she convinced her-self it was because she would be leaving soon, return-ing to Denver. Then there would be no reason for their paths to cross again. If things worked out between the Westmorelands and the Outlaws, she could see Walker hanging out with her brothers and cousins every now and then, but she doubted she would be invited to attend any of those gatherings.

Knowing he was waiting for an answer, she said, "Yes, I'll share lunch with you."

Ten

"So, Bailey, who taught you how to shoot?"

She bit into her sandwich and held up her finger to let him know it would be a minute before she could answer because she had food in her mouth. Walker didn't mind watching her anyway.

"The question you should probably ask is who *didn't* teach me to shoot. My brothers and cousins were quick to give me lessons, especially Bane. He's so good that he's a master sniper with the navy SEALs. Bane taught me how to hit a target. I don't want to sound as if I'm bragging, but I'm an excellent shot because of him."

"You're not bragging, just stating a fact. I'm living proof, and note I said *living* proof. There's no doubt in my mind that grizzly would have done me in if you hadn't taken it down."

"Well, I'm glad I was there."

He was glad she'd been there, too. At the sight of a huge grizzly any other woman would have gone into shock. But not Bailey. She had showed true grit by bringing down that bear. She'd made that shot from a distance he doubted even he could have made. His three men had admitted they could not have made it without running the risk of shooting him.

"My men are in awe of you," he added. "You impressed them."

She frowned. "I didn't do it to impress anyone, Walker. I did what I felt I had to do. I wasn't going after accolades."

That, he thought, was what made her different. Most of the women he knew would use anything to score brownie points. Hadn't making a good impression meant everything to Kalyn?

"I think you're the real hero, Walker. You risked your life getting that bear away from the shack before it got to Marcus."

He shrugged. "Like you said, I did what I felt I had to do. I wasn't going after accolades." He blinked over at her and smiled. He was rewarded when she smiled back.

Just what was he doing flirting with her? He was pretty rusty at it. There hadn't been a woman he'd really been attracted to since Kalyn. He'd had meaningless affairs solely for the purpose of quenching raging hormones, but he hadn't been interested in a woman beyond sex...until now.

He bit into his sandwich. "This is good. I hope I didn't get underfoot while you prepared lunch, but I couldn't stay in my bedroom a minute longer."

"Thanks, and no, you didn't get underfoot."

But he had made her nervous, he was sure of it. She'd been leaning over looking into the refrigerator when he'd walked into the kitchen. The sight of her sweats stretched over a curvy bottom had definitely increased his testosterone level. He had been happy just to stand there, leaning against the kitchen counter with an erection, and stare. After closing the refrigerator she'd nearly dropped the jars of mayo and mustard when she'd turned around to find him there. Of course she'd scolded him for coming down the stairs without her assistance, but he'd ignored all that. He wasn't used to a woman fussing over him.

She'd made him sit down at the table and had given him a magazine that had been delivered by the mailman earlier. Instead of flipping through the pages, he'd preferred watching her move around the kitchen. More than once she'd caught him staring and he'd quickly glanced back down at the magazine.

Walker would be the first to admit he'd picked up on a difference in the atmosphere of his home. It now held the scent of a woman. Although the guest room she was using was on the opposite side of the house, the moment he'd walked out of his bedroom, the scent of jasmine had flowed through his nostrils. At first he'd been taken off guard by it but then he decided he preferred it to the woodsy smell he was used to. It was then that he realized someone other than himself occupied the house for the first time since his parents' deaths. His privacy had been invaded, but, surprisingly, he didn't have a problem with it. Bailey had a way of growing on a person.

"Will you be returning to your room after you finish lunch?" she asked.

He glanced over at her. "No. There're a few things I need to do."

"Like what?"

He lifted a brow. Did she think whatever he did was any of her business?

As if she read his mind, she said, "I hope you're not planning to do anything that might cause a setback, Walker."

He heard the concern in her voice and clearly saw it in her eyes. It reminded him of what had been missing in his life for almost ten years. A woman who cared.

A woman he desired.

Although they had never made love, they had come close. It didn't take much to remember a pair of perfectly shaped breasts or the wetness of her femininity. Going down on a woman wasn't part of his regular lovemaking routine, but Bailey's scent had made him want to do it for her, and after that first time he'd found her flavor addictive.

So yes, he desired her. With a passion. Whenever he saw her, his mind filled with all the things he'd love to do to her. It had been a long time since he'd slept with a woman, but that wasn't the issue. He desired Bailey simply because she was a woman worthy of desiring. There had been this attraction between them from the start, and they both knew it. The attraction was still alive and kicking, and they both knew that, as well.

How long were they planning to play the "try to ignore it" game?

"No setbacks for me. I intend to follow Dr. Witherspoon's orders."

"Good."

Did Bailey realize she liked getting in the last word? "I need to go over my books, replenish my stock and order more branding equipment. I'll be fine."

She nodded before getting up from the table. She reached for his plate and he placed his hand on hers. He immediately felt a sizzle race up his spine and he fought to ignore it. "I can take care of my own plate. I appreciate you being here but I don't want you to feel as if you have to wait on me. I'm doing better."

What he didn't add was that he was doing well enough for her to go back home to Westmoreland Country. However, for reasons he wasn't ready to question, her leaving was not what he wanted.

"Fine," she said, moving away from the table.

He tried concentrating on his cup of coffee, but couldn't.

He watched her move around the room, putting stuff away. He enjoyed watching how her body looked in sweats. Whenever she moved, so did his sex as it tingled with need.

"Any reason you're staring?" she asked, turning to meet his gaze.

She looked younger today. Softer. It could be the way the daylight was coming in through the window. "You got eyes in the back of your head, Bailey?"

"No, but I could feel you staring."

In that case there was no need to lie. "Yes, I was staring. You look good in that outfit."

She looked down at herself. "In sweats? You've got to be kidding me. You must have taken an extra pill or two this morning."

He smiled as his gaze raked over her. "No, I didn't take an extra pill or two. Just stating the facts."

He sensed she didn't believe him. She brushed her fingers through her hair as if his comment had given her reason to wonder if she looked just the opposite. Possibly disheveled and unkempt. He found that interesting. How could she not know she looked good no matter what she wore? And she probably had no idea that her hot, lush scent filled the kitchen instead of the scent of what she'd prepared for lunch.

As if dismissing what he'd said, she turned back to the sink. "Are you going to sit there and stare or are you going to work in your office?" she asked over her shoulder a few moments later.

"I think I'll just sit here and stare for a while."

"It's not nice to stare."

"So I've heard."

She swung around and frowned at him. "Then, stare at something else, Walker."

A smile touched the corner of his lips. "There's noth-

ing else in this kitchen I would rather stare at than you."
And he meant it.

"Sounds as if you've got a case of cabin fever."

"Possibly, but I doubt it."

She placed the dish towel on the counter. "So what do
you think it is?"

He placed his coffee cup down, thinking that was easy
enough to answer. "Lust. I'm lusting after you, Bailey."

A drugging urgency slammed into Bailey's chest, making her nipples pucker and fire race through her veins.
Now, more than before, she felt the weight of Walker's
gaze. She didn't usually feel feminine in sweats, but he
had a way of making her feel sexy even when she didn't
have a right to feel that way.

And while he sat there, watching her every move, she
was fully aware of what was going through his mind. Because she was pretty certain it was the same thing going
through hers. This seductive heat was beginning to affect
her everywhere—in her breasts, deep in the juncture of
her thighs and in the middle of her stomach. The memories of those two kisses they'd previously shared only
intensified the hot, aching sensations overwhelming her
common sense.

She heard him slide the chair back and watched as he
slowly stood. "You can come here or I'm coming over
there," he said matter-of-factly in a deep voice.

She swallowed, knowing he was serious. As serious as
she was hot for him. But was she ready for this? A meaningless affair with Walker? Hadn't he told her that night
in the truck at Bailey's Bay that all he could offer was a
meaningless affair? At the time, she'd responded by saying that kind of relationship didn't bother her. Her future
was tied to Westmoreland Country and not to any man.
There wasn't that much love in the world.

But there was that much passion. That much desire. To a degree she'd never encountered before. She couldn't understand it, but there was no denying the way her body responded to him. It responded in a way it had never reacted to another man. A part of her believed this was no accident. What was taking place between them was meant to be. Not only was that thought a discovery, it was also an acceptance.

It was that acceptance that pushed her to say, "Meet me halfway."

He nodded and moved toward her. She moved toward him. Bailey drew in a deep breath with every step, keeping her gaze fixed on his face. That strong, square chin, those gorgeous dark eyes, his delicious mouth. He was such a striking figure of a man whose looks alone could make a woman shiver. Toss in her nightly naughty dreams and it made her bold enough to turn those dreams into reality.

When they met in the center of the kitchen, he wrapped his arms around her with a possessiveness that took her breath away.

"Be careful of your leg," she warned softly after managing to breathe again. She liked the feel of his body pressed hard against hers.

"My leg isn't what's aching," he said with a huskiness she heard. "Something else is."

She knew what that something else was. She could feel his erection pressed against the juncture of her thighs. Even while recovering from his injury, his strength amazed her. Although he annoyed her at times by not asking for help, his willpower and independence were admirable. And the thought that this was one particular area where this strong, sexy specimen of a man *did* need her sent her mind and body soaring.

He pulled back slightly to look down at her and she almost melted from the heat in his eyes. The feel of him cupping her bottom to keep their middles connected wasn't helping matters. "Our first time making love should be in a bed, Bailey. But I'm not sure I can make it that far. I need you now," he said in a voice filled with need.

"I'm okay with that, Walker. I need you now, too." She was being honest with him. When it came to sex, she felt honesty was the best policy. She detested the lies and games some couples played.

He pulled her back into his arms when he said, "There's something I need to warn you about."

Now she was the one to pull back slightly to look up at him. "What?"

"It's been a long time since I've been with a woman. A few years. About five."

The information, which he hadn't had to give her, tugged at something deep inside her. "It's been a long time since I've been with a man, as well. More than five years."

He smiled and she knew why. She'd been around the males in her family long enough to know they had no problems with double standards. They could sleep around but didn't want to know their women had done the same.

She wrapped her arms around his neck. "What about your leg? How do you plan for this to work? Got any ideas?"

"I've got plenty and I plan to try out every last one of them."

His words made her heart pound hard against her chest. "Bring it on, Walker Rafferty."

"Baby, I intend to do just that." And then he lowered his mouth down to hers.

Eleven

Sensation ripped through Walker the moment their mouths connected. He eased his tongue into her mouth and kissed her with a hunger that had her groaning. In response his erection pressed even harder against his zipper.

He captured her tongue with his and did the kinds of erotic things he'd dreamed of doing. He sucked as if the need to taste her was as essential to him as breathing. He deepened the kiss and tightened his arms around her. She tasted of heat and a wildness that he found delectable.

But then he found everything about her delectable— the way she fit in his arms, the way their bodies melded together like that was the way they were supposed to be.

Walker slowly eased away from her mouth and drew in a deep satisfying breath, missing the feel of her already. "Take off your clothes," he whispered against her lips.

She raised a brow. "In here?"

He smiled. "Yes. I want to make love to you here. We'll try out all the other rooms later."

She chuckled. "Horny, aren't we?"

He leaned in and licked her lips. "Like I said, it's been five years."

"In that case…"

Moving out of his arms, she took a few steps back and began removing her clothes. He watched her every move, getting more turned on with each stitch she discarded. When she had stripped down to nothing but her panties and bra, he finally released the breath he'd been holding.

He was weak in the knees from looking at her and he leaned against the breakfast bar for support. He needed it when she removed her bra and then slowly peeled her panties down her thighs. He couldn't help growling in pleasure.

It was only then he remembered something very important.

"Damn."

She lifted a concerned brow. "What's wrong?"

"Condoms. I don't have any down here. They're upstairs in my nightstand."

She shook her head. "No need, unless you're concerned about it for health reasons. I'm on the pill to regulate my periods."

He nodded. The thought of spilling inside her sent all kinds of luscious sensations through him. "No concerns. I'm okay with it, if you are."

"I'm okay with it."

He couldn't help but rake his gaze over her naked body. "You are beautiful, Bailey. From the top of your head to your pretty little feet, you are absolutely beautiful."

Bailey had never allowed any man's compliments to go to her head…until now. Walker sounded so serious and the look on his face was so sincere that her heart pounded in appreciation. She wasn't sure why his opinion of how she looked mattered, but it did. And she immediately thought of a way to thank him. Reclaiming the distance separating them, she leaned up on her toes and brushed her lips across his. Then she licked a line from one corner of his mouth to the other in a slow and provocative way.

She smiled in pleasure when she heard his quick intake of breath, glad to know she was getting to him as much as he was getting to her. "Now for your clothes, Walker, and I intend to help you." She intended to do more than that but he would find that out soon enough. He braced against the breakfast bar as she bent down to remove his shoes and socks.

Now for his shirt. She leaned forward and undid the buttons while occasionally leaning up to nip and lick his mouth. The more he moaned the bolder she got as she assisted him out of his shirt and then his T-shirt.

Wow, what a chest. She ran her fingers through the coarse hair covering it. She loved the feel of it beneath her hands. She trailed kisses from his lips, past his jawline to his chest and then used her teeth to nibble on his nipples before devouring them with her tongue and lips.

"Bailey." He breathed out her name in a forced whisper. "I need you."

She needed him, too, but first...

She reached down and unsnapped his jeans before easing down his zipper. Then she inserted her hand into the opening to cup him. She smiled at how thick he felt in her hand. "Um, I think we should get rid of your jeans and briefs, don't you?"

Instead of giving him a chance to answer, she kissed him again, using her tongue to further stir the passion between them. She heard him moan, which was followed by a deep growl when she sucked on his lower lip.

"Don't think I can handle this much longer," he said through clenched teeth.

"Oh, I think you can handle more than you think you can, Walker. Let's see."

She helped him remove his jeans and briefs and then stood back and raked her gaze over him before meeting his eyes. "You are so buff. So gorgeously handsome. So—"

Before she could finish he pulled her to him, capturing her lips in an openmouthed kiss as raw as it was possessive. And when she felt his hand between her legs, she broke off the kiss to ease out of his arms.

"Not so fast. I'm a guest in your home, so today I get to have my way," she whispered.

With that, her fingers gripped his hardness and gently squeezed, loving the feel of his bare flesh in her hands.

"Don't torture me, baby."

Torture? He hadn't endured any torture yet, she thought, as she continued to fondle his thick width, texture and length, loving every minute of it. He was huge, and she intended to sample every single inch.

In a move she knew he was not expecting, she dropped down on her knees and took him into the warmth of her mouth.

"Bailey!"

Walker grabbed her head but instead of pulling her mouth away, he wrapped his fingers in the locks of her hair. He lost all control while watching her head bob up and down. Every muscle in his body trembled and his insides shivered with the impact of her mouth on him. She was pushing him deliciously over the edge. He felt ready to explode.

It was then that he tugged on her hair, using enough force to pull her mouth from him. She looked up at him and smiled, licking her lips. "I need to get inside you now," he said in a guttural growl. He had reached his limit.

In a surprise move, he pulled her up and lifted her to sit on the kitchen table, spreading her legs wide in the process.

Thanks to her, his control was shot to hell. He trailed his fingers through the curls surrounding her feminine folds. She wasn't the only one who wanted a taste. He lowered his head to her wetness.

"Walker!"

He ignored her screaming his name as his tongue devoured her as she'd done to him. And when she wrapped her legs around his neck and bucked her hips against his mouth he knew he was giving her a taste of her own medicine.

When he'd pushed her far enough, he spread her legs farther, positioned his body between them and thrust until he was fully embedded within her. Then he held tight to her hips as he went deeper with every plunge.

Something inside him snapped, and his body moved with the speed of a jackhammer. When she wrapped her legs around his waist he threw his head back and filled his nostrils with her scent.

They came together, him holding tight to her hips. Why this felt so right, he wasn't sure. All he knew was that it did. He needed this. He needed her. And from the sounds of her moans, she needed him.

They were both getting what they needed.

Bailey came awake and shifted in Walker's arms, recalling how they'd made it out of the kitchen to the sofa in his living room. She eased up and tried to move off him when she remembered his leg.

His arms held tight around her like a band of steel. "Where do you think you're going?"

She looked down at him and remembered why he was down there and she was on top. Upon his encouragement, she had shown him that she wasn't only a good shot. She was a pretty damn good rider, as well.

She glanced at the clock. It was close to eight. They had slept almost through dinner. Okay, she would admit they hadn't slept the entire time. They had slept in between their many rounds of lovemaking.

"Your leg," she reminded him, holding his gaze.

He had a sexy, sluggish look in his eyes.

"My leg is fine."

"It's after eight and you didn't take your medicine at five."

A smile curved his lips. "I had another kind of medicine that I happen to like better."

She shook her head. "Tell that to your leg when it starts hurting later."

"Trust me, I will. Making love to you is better than any medicine Doc Witherspoon could have prescribed for me." And then he pulled her mouth down to his and kissed her in a slow, unhurried fashion that clouded her mind. She was grateful for the ringing of her cell phone until she recognized the ringtone.

She broke off the kiss and quickly scooted off Walker to grab her phone off the coffee table, being careful not to bump his leg. "Dillon! What's going on?"

"Hey, Bay. I was calling to check to see how Walker is doing."

She glanced over at Walker who was stretched out naked on the sofa. She licked her lips and then said to Dillon, "Walker is doing fine. Improving every day. The doctor is pleased with his progress."

"That's good to hear. And how are you doing? Is it cold enough there for you?"

"Yes, I'm doing good," she said, glancing down at her own naked body. It was a good thing Dillon had no idea just how good she was doing. "There was a bad snow-storm here."

"I heard about that. You took plenty of heavy clothing didn't you?"

"Yes, I'm good."

"You most certainly are," Walker whispered.

She gave Walker a scolding glance, hoping Dillon hadn't heard what Walker had said.

"Do you have any idea when you'll be coming back home?" Dillon asked.

She swallowed hard and switched her gaze from Walker to the window when she said, "No, I don't know when I'll be back. I don't want to leave Walker too soon. But when the doctor says Walker can handle things on his own, I'll be back."

"All right. Give Walker my regards and tell him the entire family is wishing him a speedy recovery."

"Okay. I'll tell him. Goodbye, Dillon."

"Goodbye, Bay."

She clicked off the phone and held it in her hand a second before placing it back on the table.

"What did Dillon want you to tell me?"

"That the family is wishing you a speedy recovery."

He nodded and pulled up into a sitting position. "That's nice of them."

She smiled and returned to the sofa to sit beside him. "I have a nice family."

"I'll have to agree with you there. You didn't say how the wedding went."

Her smile widened. "It was wonderful and Jill made a beautiful bride. I don't know who cried the most, Jill, Pam or their other two sisters." She paused and then added, "Ian, Reggie and Quade hated they didn't get the chance to meet you."

"And I hate I didn't get the chance to meet them."

She couldn't help but remember he'd left because of her. She looked at him. "Do you think you'll ever return to Denver to visit?"

Walker captured the back of her neck with his hand and brought her mouth closer to his. He nibbled around her lips before placing an openmouthed kiss on her neck. "Um, will you make it worth my while if I do?"

She closed her eyes, loving the way Walker ravished her with his mouth and tongue. Desire coiled in her stomach. "I can't make any promises, but I'll see what I can do."

He pulled back slightly and she opened her eyes and met his gaze. She saw a serious glint in the dark depths as he said, "Dillon asked when you were coming home."

He'd presented it as a statement and not a question. "Yes. I told him when you got better."

He nodded, holding fast to her gaze. "I'm better."

Bailey drew in a deep breath, wondering if he was telling her that because he was ready for her to leave. "Have I worn out my welcome?"

He gently gripped her wrist and brought it to his lips, placing a light kiss on her skin. "I don't think that's possible."

She decided not to remind him he was a loner. A man who preferred solitude to company. "In that case, I'll stay another week."

He flashed a sexy smile. "Or two?"

She tried not to blink in surprise that he was actually suggesting she hang around for two weeks instead of one. She glided her hand across the firmness of his jaw. "Yes. Or two."

As if he was satisfied with her answer, he leaned in and opened his mouth against hers.

Twelve

Walker left his bathroom and glanced across the room at his bed and the woman in it. This was the third night she'd spent with him and it was hard to remember a time when she hadn't. A part of him didn't want to remember it.

He rubbed a hand down his face. Bailey in his bed was something he shouldn't get used to. It was countdown time, and in a little less than two weeks she'd be gone and his life would return to normal.

Normal meant living for himself and nobody else. Garth often teased him about living a miserable life. Misery didn't need company. *He* didn't need company, but Bailey had made him realize that five years had been too long to go without a woman. He was enjoying her in his bed a little too damn much. And that unfortunately wasn't the crux of his problem. The real kicker was that he was enjoying her...even without the sex.

He hadn't gotten around to working until yesterday, and she had found what she claimed was the perfect spot in his office to sit and work on the laptop she had brought with her. That way she was still connected to her job in Denver.

They had worked in amicable silence, although he'd been fully aware of her the entire time. Her presence had made him realize what true loneliness was because he didn't want to think of a time when she wouldn't be there.

Forcing that thought to the back of his mind, he moved across the room to rekindle the flames in the fireplace. While jabbing at the wood with the poker, he glanced back over his shoulder when he heard Bailey shift around. She looked small in his huge bed. She looked good. As if she belonged.

He quickly turned back to the fire, forcing his thoughts off her and onto something else. Like Morris James's visit yesterday. The rancher had wanted to meet Bailey after hearing all about her. Word of how she'd downed that bear had spread quickly, far and wide. Morris wanted to present Bailey with the ten-thousand-dollar bounty she'd earned from killing the animal.

Bailey had refused to take it and instead told Morris she wanted to donate the money to charity, especially if there was one in town that dealt with kids. The surprised look on Morris's face had been priceless. What person in her right mind gives up ten thousand dollars? But both Walker and Morris had watched her sign the paperwork to do just that.

As he continued to jab the poker in the fire another Bailey moment came to mind. He recalled the day he'd stepped out onto his front porch for the first time in a week. While sipping a cup of coffee he'd watched in fascination as Bailey had built a snowman. And when she'd invited him to help her, he had. He hadn't done something like that since he was a kid and he had to admit he'd enjoyed it.

For a man who didn't like having his privacy invaded, not only had she invaded that privacy, but for the time being she was making privacy nonexistent. Like when he'd come downstairs for breakfast this morning to find all four of his men sitting at his table. Somehow she'd discovered it was Willie's birthday and she'd wanted to do something special. At first Walker had been a little annoyed that she'd done such a thing without confiding in him, but then he realized that was Bailey's way—to do as she pleased. He couldn't help but smile at that.

But then he frowned upon realizing it was also Bailey's way to be surrounded by people. Although he was used to loneliness, she was not. She had a big family and was used to having people around all the time. He figured the loneliness of Alaska would eventually drive her crazy. What if she decided to leave before the two weeks?

Why should he give a damn if she did?

He returned the poker to the stand, not wanting to think about that. He was expecting another visit from Doc Witherspoon tomorrow. Hopefully it would be his last for a while. He couldn't wait to take out his plane and fly over his land. And he didn't want to question why he wanted Bailey with him to share in the experience.

"Walker?"

He glanced across the room. Bailey was sitting up in his bed. Her hair was mussed up and she had a soft, sleepy and sexy look on her face. Although she held the covers up to her chest, she looked tempting. Maybe because he knew that beneath all those bedcovers she was naked. "Yes?"

"I'm cold."

"I just finished stoking the fire."

"Not good enough, Alaskan. I'm sure you can do better than that."

Oh, yes, he definitely could. He removed his robe and headed for the bed, feeling a deep ache in his groin. The moment he slid in bed and felt her thigh brush against his, the ache intensified. He pulled her into his arms, needing to hold her. He knew there would come a time when he wouldn't be able to do that. The thought had him drawing in a deep, ragged breath.

She pulled back and ran her gaze over his face. "You okay?"

"Yes."

"Your leg?"

"Is fine. Back to the way it used to be. Only lasting reminder is that little scar."

"Trust me, Walker, no woman will care about that scar when you've got this to back things up," she said, reaching her hand beneath the covers to cup him, then stroke him. Walker drew in another ragged breath. Bailey definitely knew how to get to the heart of the matter. And when he saw the way she licked her lips and how the darkness of her eyes shone with desire, his erection expanded in her hand.

She leaned close to his ear and whispered, "Okay, Walker, what's it going to be? You ride me or I ride you? Take your pick."

He couldn't stop the smile that curved his lips. It was hard—damn difficult, outright impossible—not to tap into all his sexual fantasies when she was around and being so damn accommodating. And she would be around for eleven more days. He intended to make the most of what he considered the best time of his life.

"Um," he said, pulling her back into his arms. "How about if we do both?"

Over the next several days Walker and Bailey settled into a gratifying and pleasurable routine. Now that Walker was back at 100 percent, he would get up every morning around five o'clock to work alongside his men. Then at nine, instead of hanging around and eating Willie's cooking like he normally did, he hightailed it back to the ranch house, where Bailey would have breakfast waiting on him. No matter how often he told her that she didn't have to go out of her way, she would wave her hand and brush off his words. After placing the most delectable-looking meal in front of him, she would go on and on about what a beautiful kitchen he had. It was one that would entice someone to cook whether they wanted to or not, she claimed.

He began to see his kitchen through her eyes and finally understood. In all the years he had lived here, he'd never thought of his kitchen, or any kitchen, as beautiful. It was a place to cook meals and eat. But she brought his attention to the space, its rustic look. But what she said she liked most was sitting at the table and looking out at the strait. On a clear day the waters looked breathtaking. Just as breathtaking as Gemma Lake, she'd told him. It was during those conversations that he knew she missed her home. Hadn't one of her rules been to never venture far from Westmoreland Country for too long?

Garth had dropped by twice to check on Walker, and because his best friend had been calling every day to see how he was doing, Garth wasn't surprised to find Bailey still there. Garth didn't seem surprised at how comfortable she'd made herself in Walker's home, either. And Walker had caught Garth staring at them with a silly-looking grin on his face more than once.

Garth had mentioned to Bailey that he'd gotten in touch with her family and had spoken to Dillon and Ramsey, and that he and his brothers would be flying to Denver in a few weeks. Bailey mentioned that she would be back home by then and that she and her family would anxiously await Garth's visit. Her comment only made Walker realize that he didn't have a lot of time left with her.

Lola was back on her regular housekeeping schedule and told him more than once how much she liked Bailey. He figured it was because Bailey was chattier with her than he'd ever been. And he figured since Lola had only one bed in the house to make up, the older woman had pretty much figured out that he and Bailey were sharing it. That had suited Lola since she'd hinted more than once that he needed a woman in his life and that being alone on the ranch wasn't good for him.

Walker took a sip of his coffee while looking out at the strait. He remembered the day Bailey had gone into town with him to pick up supplies. News of her and the bear had spread further than Walker had imagined it would, and she'd become something of a legend. And if that wasn't enough, Morris had spread the word about what she'd done with the bounty money. Her generous contribution had gone to Kodiak Way, the local orphanage. Walker hadn't visited the place in years, not since he'd gone there on a field trip with his high school. But he'd decided on that particular day to stop by with Bailey, so she could see where her money had gone.

It had amazed him how taken she'd been with all the children, but he really should not have been surprised. He recalled how much she adored her nieces, nephews and little cousins back in Denver and just how much they'd adored her. He and Bailey had spent longer at the orphanage than he had planned because Bailey couldn't miss the opportunity to take a group of kids outside to build a snowman.

He then recalled the day he'd taken her up in his single-engine plane, giving her a tour of his land. She had been in awe and had told him how beautiful his property was. When she'd asked him how he'd learned to fly, he'd opened up and told her of his and Garth's time together in the marines. She'd seemed fascinated by everything he told her and he'd gotten caught up in her interest.

It had been a beautiful day for flying. The sky had

been blue and the clouds a winter white. From the air he had pointed out his favorite areas—the lakes, small coves, hidden caves and mountaintops. And he'd heard himself promising to one day cover the land with her in his Jeep.

And then there had been the day when she'd pulled him into his office, shoved him down into the chair at his desk and proceeded to sit in his lap so she could show him what she'd downloaded on his desktop computer. Jillian and Aidan had returned from their three-week honeymoon to France, Italy and Spain, and had uploaded their wedding video. Bailey thought that since he'd missed the wedding, he could watch the video.

As far as weddings went, it had been a nice one. Bailey had pointed out several cousins he hadn't met and their wives and children. He agreed that Jillian had been a beautiful bride and he'd seen the love in Aidan's eyes when she'd walked down the aisle on Dillon's arm.

Watching the video made Walker recall his own wedding. Only thing, his wedding had been nothing more than a circus. His parents and Garth had tried to warn him with no luck. A few nights ago he'd dreamed about Kalyn and Connor. A dream that had turned into a nightmare, with Bailey waking him up.

The next day, even though he'd seen the probing curiosity in her eyes, she hadn't asked him about it and he hadn't felt the need to tell her.

Walker took another sip of his coffee and glanced down at his watch. Bailey should be coming down for breakfast any minute. He had finished his chores with the men earlier than usual and had rushed back to the ranch house. More than once he'd been tempted to go upstairs and wake her but he knew if he did they might end up staying in bed the rest of the day. He then thought about the phone call he'd received an hour ago from Charm. It seemed Charm couldn't wait to meet her look-alike and asked that he fly Bailey to Fairbanks this weekend. He hadn't made any promises, but he'd told her he would talk to Bailey about it.

Moments later, he heard her upstairs and felt his sex stir in anticipation. Only Bailey could put him in such a state, arousing him so easily and completely. And he would admit that her mere presence in his home brought him a kind of joy he hadn't thought he would ever feel again.

But then he also knew it was the kind of joy he couldn't allow himself to get attached to. Just as sure as he knew that when he got up every morning the strait would be filled with water, he knew that when Bailey's days were up, she would be leaving.

Already he'd detected a longing in her and figured she'd become homesick. It was during those times that he was reminded of the first day they'd met. She'd told him about her rules and her love for Westmoreland Country. She'd said she never intended to leave it. And since he never intended to leave Kodiak, that meant any wishful thinking about them spending their lives together was a waste of his time.

Walker's grip on the cup tightened. And hadn't she told him about men getting possessive, becoming territorial and acting crazy sometimes? Sadly, he could now see himself doing all three where she was concerned.

It was nobody's fault but his own that he was now in this state. He'd known her rules and had allowed her to get under his skin anyway. But he could handle it. He had no choice. He would store up memories of the good times, and those memories would get him through the lonely nights after she left.

He heard her moving around upstairs again and sat his coffee cup down. Temptation was ruling his senses now.

Desire unlike anything he'd ever felt before took control of him, had him sliding back from the table and standing.

` Walker left the kitchen and moved quickly toward the stairs, seeking the object of his craving.

Thirteen

"What am I going to do, Josette? Of all the stupid, idiotic, crazy things I could have done, why did I fall in love with Walker Rafferty?" Bailey asked. She held her mobile phone to her ear and paced Walker's bedroom. Talk about doing something dumb.

She had woken up that morning and glanced out the window on her way to the bathroom. She'd seen Walker and his men in the distance, knee deep in snow, loading some type of farm equipment onto a truck. She had stared at him, admiring how good he looked even dressed in a heavy coat and boots with a hat on his head. All she could think about was the night before, how he had made love to her, how he'd made her scream a number of times. And how this morning before leaving the bed he had brushed a good-morning kiss across her lips.

Suddenly, while standing at the window and ogling him, it had hit her—hard—that all those emotions she'd been feeling lately weren't lust. They were love.

She had fallen head over heels in love with Walker.

"Damn it, Josette. I should have known better."

"Calm down, Bailey. There's nothing stupid, idiotic or crazy about falling in love."

"It is if the man you love has no intention of ever loving you back. Walker told me all he could ever offer is a meaningless affair. I knew that and fell in love with him anyway."

"What makes you think he hasn't changed his mind? Now that the two of you have spent time together at his ranch, he might have."

"I have no reason to think he won't be ready for me to leave when my two weeks are up. Especially after that stunt I pulled the other day. Inviting his men for breakfast without his permission. Although he didn't say anything, I could tell he didn't like it."

"Are you going to tell him how you feel?"

"Of course not! Do you want me to feel even more stupid?"

"So what are you going to do?"

Bailey paused, not knowing how she intended to answer that. And also knowing there was really only one way to answer it. "Nothing. Just enjoy the time I have with him now and leave with no regrets. I believe the reason he refuses to love anyone else is because he's still carrying a torch for his late wife. There's nothing I can do about that and I don't intend to try."

Moments later, after ending her phone call with Josette, Bailey walked back over to the window. Today the weather appeared clearer than it had been the past couple of days. She missed home, but not as much as she'd figured she would. Skype had helped. She communicated regularly with her nieces and nephews and little cousins and, according to Ramsey, although several wives were expecting new babies in the family, none had been born.

Everyone was expecting her home for Thanksgiving and was looking forward to her return.

She had worked out a system with Lucia where she could work remotely from Alaska. Doing so helped fill the long days when Walker was gone. In the evenings she looked forward to his return. Although they had established an amicable routine, she knew it was just temporary. Like she'd told Josette, there was no doubt in her mind Walker would expect her to leave next week. Granted, she knew he enjoyed her as his bedmate, but she also knew that, for men, sex was nothing more than sex. She had found that out while watching her then-single Westmoreland brothers and cousins. For her and Walker, there could never be anything between them other than the physical.

Even so, she could sense there was something bothering Walker. More than once she'd awakened in the night to find him standing at the window or poking the fire. And then there had been the night he'd woken up screaming the words, "No, Kalyn! Don't! Connor! Connor!"

She had snuggled closer and wrapped her arms around him, and pretty soon he had calmed down, holding her as tightly as she held him. The next day over breakfast she had expected him to bring up the incident, but he hadn't. She could only assume he didn't remember it or didn't want to talk about it. But she had been curious enough to check online and she'd found out Kalyn had been his wife and Connor his son.

Bailey turned when she heard the bedroom door opening, and there Walker stood, looking more handsome than any man had a right to look. As she stood there staring, too mesmerized by the heat in his eyes to even speak, he closed the door and removed his jacket, then tossed it across the chair.

She'd seen that look in his eyes before, usually in the evenings after he'd spent the entire day on the range. It wasn't quite nine in the morning. She swallowed. Now he was unbuttoning his shirt. "Good morning, Walker."

"Good morning, Bailey." He pulled the belt from his jeans before sitting in the chair to remove his boots and socks. His eyes never left hers.

"You've finished your chores for the day already?"

"No."

"No?"

"Yes, no. The guys took my tractor over to the Mayeses' place for Conley to look at it. He's the area mechanic. Nothing much to do until they get back, which won't be for hours."

She nodded. "I see."

"I came in for coffee and had a cup before hearing you move around up here, letting me know you were awake." Now he was unzipping his pants.

"And?" she asked, as if she really didn't know.

He slid his pants down muscular thighs. "And—" he crooked his finger "—come here a minute."

He stood there stark naked. She couldn't help licking her lips as her gaze moved from his eyes downward, past his chest to the thatch of dark hair covering his erection. "Before or after I take off my clothes?" she asked.

"Before. I want to undress you."

At that moment she didn't care that she'd just finished putting on her clothes. From the look in his eyes, he was interested in more than just taking off her clothes.

Drawing in a deep breath and trying to ignore the throb between her legs, she crossed the room on wobbly knees. Was she imagining things or was his erection expanding with each step she took? When she stopped in front of him, he placed both hands on her shoulders. She felt the heat of his touch through her blouse.

"You look good in this outfit," he said, holding fast to her shoulders as his gaze raked over her.

"Thanks." It was just a skirt and blouse. Nothing spectacular.

"You're welcome." Then he captured her lips with his. Her last coherent thought was *But this kiss* is *spectacular.*

Walker was convinced, and had been for some time, that Bailey was what fantasies were made of. What he'd told her was the truth. She looked good in that outfit. Truth be told, she looked good in any outfit...especially in his shirts. Those were the times he felt most possessive, territorial, crazy with lust...and love. All the things that she'd once stated were total turnoffs for her.

He continued kissing her, moving his mouth over her lips with a hunger he felt all the way to his toes. He had wanted this kiss to arouse her, get her ready for what was to come. He figured she knew his motives because of the way she was responding. Their tongues tangled madly, greedily, as hot and intense as it could get.

His hands left her shoulders and cupped her backside, pressing her body against his. There was no way she didn't feel his erection pressing against the juncture of her thighs.

He'd watched her crossing the room and noticed her gaze shifting from his face to his groin, checking him out. He really didn't know why. Nothing about that part of his body had changed. She had cupped it, taken it into her mouth and fondled it. So what had she found so fascinating about it today?

As if she'd guessed his thoughts, she glanced up to meet his eyes just seconds before reaching him. The tint that darkened her cheeks had been priceless, and instead of stripping her clothes off like he'd intended, he kissed her. He'd overplayed his hand with Bailey. This young woman had done what no other could have done. She was on the verge of making him whole. Making him want to believe in love all over again. Restoring his soul to what it had been before Kalyn had destroyed it.

He slowly broke off the kiss. His hands returned to her shoulders only long enough to remove her blouse and un-hook her bra. And then he tugged her skirt and panties down past her hips and legs to pool at her feet. He looked his fill. Now he understood her earlier fascination with him because he was experiencing the same fascination now.

Yes, he'd seen it all before. Had tasted and touched every single inch. But still, looking at her naked body al-most took his breath away. She was beautiful. His body ached for her in a way it had never ached for another woman...including Kalyn.

That realization had him lifting her into his arms, car-rying her to the bed. He placed her on it and joined her there. He had intended to go slow, to savor each moment as long as he could. But she had other ideas.

When they stretched out together on the huge bed, her mouth went for his and kissed him hungrily. The same way he'd kissed her moments ago. The only difference was that her hands were everywhere, touching, exploring and strok-ing. He joined in with his own hands, frenzied with the need to touch her and let his mouth follow. She squirmed against him, biting his shoulders a few times and licking his chest, trying to work her mouth downward. But he beat her to the punch. She released a gasp when he tightened his hold on her hips and lowered his head between her legs.

He'd only intended to lick her a few times, but her taste made that impossible. He wanted more, needed more, and he was determined to get everything he wanted.

He heard her moans, felt her nails dig deep into his shoulders. He knew the moment her pleasure came, when she was consumed in an orgasm that had her writhing be-neath his mouth.

Lust ripped through him, triggered by her moans. He

had to be inside her now. Easing his body over hers, their gazes held as he slowly entered her. It took all his strength not to explode right when she arched her back and lifted her hips to receive every last inch of him. She entwined her arms around his neck and then, in a surprise move, she leaned up slightly and traced his lips with the tip of her tongue.

Something snapped inside him and he began thrusting in and out of her, going deeper with every downward plunge. Over and over, he fine-tuned the rhythm, whipping up sensation after exquisite sensation.

"Walker!"

When she screamed his name, the same earthshaking orgasm that overtook her did the same to him. A fierce growl escaped his lips when he felt her inner muscles clench him, trying to hold him inside.

This was how it was supposed to be. Giving instead of taking. Sharing instead of just being a recipient.

When their bodies had gone limp, he found the strength to ease off her and pull her into his arms, needing to hold her close to his heart. A part of him wished they could remain like that forever, but he knew they couldn't. Time was not on their side.

He knew her rules, especially the one about staying in Westmoreland Country. And he knew the promise he'd made to his father, about never taking Hemlock Row for granted again. That meant that even if Bailey agreed to a long-term affair, there would be no compromise on either of their parts.

Even so, he was determined to stock up on all the memories he could.

"Charm called."

Bailey's body felt weak as water but somehow she managed to open her eyes and meet Walker's gaze. She was convinced the man had more stamina than a bull. And wasn't she seven years younger? He should be flat on his back barely able to move…like her.

She found the strength to draw in a slow breath. Evidently he was telling her this for a reason and there was only one way to find out what it was. "And?"

"And she asked me to bring you to Fairbanks this weekend. Let me rephrase that. She kind of ordered me to."

Bailey couldn't help but chuckle. "Ordered. I didn't think anyone had the nerve to order you to do anything."

"Charm thinks she can. She considers me one of her brothers and she thinks she can wrap all of us around her finger. Like you do with your brothers and cousins."

That got another chuckle from her. "I don't know about that anymore." When he eased down beside her, she snuggled against him. "So are you going to do it? Are you going to take me to Fairbanks?"

He looked over at her. "I thought you didn't want to have anything to do with the Outlaws."

"I never said that. I just didn't like how they handled their business by sending you to Denver instead of coming themselves." Reaching up, she entwined her arms around his neck. "But I'm over that now. If they hadn't sent you, then we would not have met."

She grimaced at the thought of that, and for the first time since meeting Walker she decided the Outlaws had definitely done her a favor. Even if he didn't love her, she now knew how it felt to fall in love with someone. To give that person your whole heart and soul. To be willing to do things you never thought you would do.

Now she understood her sisters. She'd always thought Megan and Gemma were plumb loco to consider living anywhere other than Westmoreland Country. Megan not so much, since she stayed in Westmoreland Country six months out of the year and spent the other six months in

Rico's hometown of Philly. But Gemma had made Australia her permanent home and only returned to Denver to visit on occasion. Megan and Gemma had chosen love over everything else. They knew home was where the heart was. Now Bailey did, too.

"You've gotten quiet on me."

She glanced over at Walker and smiled. "Only because you haven't answered my question. So are you going to take me to Fairbanks?" She knew that was a big request to make, because he'd mentioned once that he rarely left his ranch.

She could tell he was considering it and then he said, "Only if you go somewhere with me tomorrow."

She lifted a brow. "Where?"

He pulled her closer. "You'll know when we get there."

She stared at him silently, mulling over his request. She was curious, but she knew she would follow him to the ends of the earth if he asked her to. "Yes, I will go with you tomorrow."

Fourteen

The next morning Walker woke up with a heavy heart, pretty much like he'd done for the past ten years. It was Connor's birthday. In the past he'd spent the day alone. Even Garth knew not to bother him on that anniversary. Yet Bailey was here, and of all things he had asked her to go to Connor's grave with him, although she had no idea where they were headed.

"You're still not going to give me a hint?" Bailey asked when he placed his Stetson on his head and then led her outside. Bundled up in her coat, boots, scarf and a Denver Broncos knitted cap, she smiled over at him. Snow covered the ground but wasn't as deep as yesterday.

He shook his head. "Don't waste your smile. You'll know when we get there." She had tried to get him to tell her last night and again this morning, but he wouldn't share. He had thoroughly enjoyed her seductive efforts, though.

"I didn't know you were so mean, Walker."

"And I've always known you were persistent, Bailey. Come on," he said, taking her gloved hand to lead her toward one of his detached garages. When he raised the door she got a peek of what was inside and almost knocked him down rushing past him.

"Wow! These babies are beauties," she said, checking out the two sleek, black-and-silver snowmobiles parked beside one of his tractors. "Are they yours?"

He nodded, leaning against the tractor. "Yes, mine and Garth's. He likes to keep his here to use whenever he comes to visit. But today, this will be our transportation to get where we're going."

"Really?" she gasped excitedly, nearly jumping up and down.

Walker couldn't ignore the contentment he felt knowing he was the one responsible for her enthusiasm. "Yes. You get to use Garth's. I asked his permission for you to do so. He figures any woman who can shoot a grizzly from one hundred feet away should certainly know how to operate one of these."

Bailey laughed. "It wasn't exactly a hundred feet away and yes, I can operate one of these. Riley has one. He loves going skiing and takes it with him when he does. None of us can understand it, but he loves cold weather. The colder the better."

Walker opened a wooden box and pulled out two visored helmets and handed her one. "Where we're going isn't far from here."

She looked up at him as she placed her helmet on her head. "And you still won't give me a hint?"

"No, not even a little one."

Of all the places Bailey figured they might end up, a cemetery wasn't even on her list. When they had brought the snowmobiles to a stop by a wooden gate she had to blink to make sure she wasn't imagining things.

Instead of asking Walker why they were there, she followed his lead and got off the machine. She watched as he opened a box connected to his snowmobile and pulled out a small broom. He then took her gloved hand in his. "This way."

Walking through snow, he led her through the opening of the small cemetery containing several headstones. They stopped in front of the first pair. "My grandparents," he said softly, releasing her hand to lean down and brush away the snow that covered the names. *Walker and Lora Rafferty.*

She glanced up at him. "You were named after your grandfather?"

He nodded. "Yes. And my father."

"So you're the third?"

He nodded again. "Yes, I'm the third. My grandfather was in the military, stationed in Fairbanks, and was sent here to the island one summer with other troops to work on a government project for a year. He fell in love with the island. He also fell in love with a young island girl he met here."

"The woman who could trace her family back to Alaska when it was owned by Russia?" Bailey asked, letting him know she remembered what he'd told her about his grandparents that first day they'd met.

A smile touched one corner of his mouth. "Yes, she's the one. They married and he bought over a thousand acres through the government land grant. He and Lora settled here and named their property Hemlock Row, after the rows of trees that are abundant on the island. They only had one child. My father."

They then moved to the second pair of headstones and she guessed this was where his parents were buried. *Walker and Darlene Rafferty.* And the one thing she noticed was that they had died within six months of each other.

She didn't want to ask but had to. "How did they die?"

At first she wasn't sure he would answer, but then his voice caught in the icy wind when he said, "Mom got sick. By the time the doctors found out it was cancer there was nothing that could be done. She loved Hemlock Row and wanted to take her last breath here. So we checked her out of the hospital and brought her home. She died less than a week later."

Bailey studied the date on the headstone. "You were here when she died?"

"Yes."

She did quick calculations in her head. Walker had lost his wife and son three months before he'd lost his mother and subsequently his father. He had fled Hollywood to come here to find peace from his grief only to face even more heartache when he'd arrived home. No wonder he'd shut himself off from the world and become a loner. He had lost the four people he'd loved the most within a year's time.

She noticed his hold on her hand tightened when he said, "Dad basically died of a broken heart. He missed Mom that much. Six months. I'm surprised he lasted without her that long. She was his heart, and I guess he figured that without her he didn't need one."

Bailey swallowed. She remembered Ramsey telling her that at least their parents had died together. He couldn't imagine one living without the other. Like Walker's, her parents had had a very close marriage.

"My father was a good one," Walker said, breaking into her thoughts. "The best. He loved Hemlock Row, and when I was a teenager he made me promise to always take care of it and keep it in the family and never sell it. I made him a promise to honor his wishes."

She nodded and recalled hearing her father and uncle had made their father and grandfathers the same such promises. That was why her family considered Westmoreland Country their home. It had been land passed to them from generation to generation. Land their great-grandfather Raphel had worked hard to own and even harder to maintain.

Walker shifted and they moved toward the next headstone. She knew before he brushed the snow off the marker who it belonged to. His son. *Connor Andrew Rafferty.*

From the dates on the headstone, he'd died four days after his first birthday, which would have been…today. She quickly glanced over at the man standing beside her, still holding her hand as he stood staring at the headstone with a solemn look on his face. Today was his son's birthday. Connor would have been eleven today.

There were no words Bailey could say because at that moment she could actually feel Walker's pain. His grief was still raw and she could tell it hadn't yet healed. So she did the only thing she could do. She leaned into him. Instead of rejecting her gesture, he placed his arms around her waist and gently drew her against his side.

They stood there together, silently gazing at the headstone. She was certain his mind was filled with memories of the son he'd lost. Long minutes passed before Walker finally spoke. "He was a good kid. Learned to walk at ten months. And he loved playing hide-and-seek."

Bailey forced a smile through the tears she tried to hold back. She bet he was a good daddy who played hide-and-seek often with his son. "Was he ever hard to find?"

Walker chuckled. "All the time. But his little giggle would always give him away."

Walker got quiet again, and then he turned her in his arms to face him. He touched her chin with his thumb. "Thanks for coming here with me today."

"Thanks for bringing me. I know today has to be painful for you."

He dropped his hand and broke eye contact to look up at the snow-covered mountains behind her. "Yes, it is every year. There are some things you just can't get over."

Bailey nodded. She then glanced around, expecting to see another headstone, and when she didn't, she gazed at Walker and asked, "Your wife?"

He looked back down at her and took her hand. "What about her?"

"Is she not buried here?"

He hesitated a moment and then said, "No." And then he tightened his hold on her hand. "Come on. Let's head back."

Later that night as Walker lay in bed holding Bailey in his arms while she slept, he thought about their time together at the cemetery. Today had been the first time he'd allowed anyone in on his emotions, his pain, the first time he'd shared his grief. And in turn, he had shared some of his family's history with her. It was history he hadn't shared with any other woman but Kalyn. The difference in how the two women had received the information had been as different as day and night.

Kalyn hadn't wanted to hear about it. Said he should forget the past and move on. She was adamant about never leaving Hollywood to return here to live. She never even visited during the three years they'd been married. How she had hated a place she'd never seen went beyond him. And she had told him that if his parents died and he inherited the place, he should sell it. She'd listed all the things they could buy with the money.

On the other hand, Bailey had listened to his family's history today and seemed to understand and appreciate everything he'd told her. She had even thanked him for sharing it with her.

He hadn't been able to verbalize his own appreciation so he'd expressed it another way. As soon as they returned to his ranch, he had whisked her into his arms, carried her up the stairs and made love to her in a way he'd never made love to any other woman.

Walker released his hold on Bailey now to ease out of bed and cross the room. He stared into the fire as if the heat actually flickered in his soul. Today, while making love to Bailey, he kept telling himself that it was only lust that made him want her so much. That it was appreciation that drove him. He refused to consider anything else. Anything more. And yet now he was fighting to maintain his resolve where she was concerned.

He didn't want or need anyone else in his life. And although he enjoyed her company now, he preferred solitude. Once she was gone, everything in his life would get back to normal. And she *would* leave, he didn't doubt that. She loved Westmoreland Country as much as he loved Hemlock Row.

He inhaled deeply, wanting to take in the smell of wood and smoke. Instead, he was filled with Bailey's scent. "Damn it, I don't want this," he uttered softly with a growl. "And I don't need her. I don't need anyone."

He released a deep breath, wondering whom he was trying to convince.

He knew the answer to that. He had to convince himself or else he'd end up making the mistake of the century, and one mistake with a woman was enough.

When Bailey had noticed Kalyn wasn't buried there, for a second he'd been tempted to confide in her. To tell her the whole sordid story about his wife and her betrayal. But he couldn't. The only living person who knew the whole story was Garth, and that was the way Walker would keep it. He could never open himself up to someone else—definitely not another woman.

He heard Bailey stirring in bed and his body responded, as usual. He wondered how long this erotic craving for her would last. He had a feeling he would have an addiction long after she was gone. But while she was here he would enjoy her and store up the memories.

"Walker?"

He turned and looked toward the bed. "I'm over here."

"I want you here."

His thoughts were pensive. He wanted to be where she was, as well. He crossed the room and eased back into bed, drawing her into his arms. They only had a few more days together and then she would be gone. She would return to Westmoreland Country without looking back. In the meantime, he would make sure the days they had together were days he could cherish forever.

Fifteen

"I don't believe it," Charm Outlaw said, caught up in a moment of awe as she stared at Bailey. "We do favor. I didn't believe Garth and Walker, but now I do." She gave Bailey a hug. "Welcome to Fairbanks, cousin."

Bailey couldn't help but smile, deciding she liked Charm right away. Everyone had been right—they did look alike. Charm's five brothers also favored their Westmoreland cousins. "Thanks for the invite. I hadn't expected all of this."

"All of this" was the dinner party Charm had planned. Walker had flown them to Fairbanks and Garth had sent a limo to pick them up from the airport. The limo had taken a route through the city's downtown. Even though a thick blanket of snow covered the grounds, Bailey thought downtown Fairbanks was almost as captivating as downtown Denver.

Walker had given her a bit of Fairbanks's history, telling her that it was a diverse city thanks to the army base there. A lot of ex-military personnel decided they liked the area and remained after their tour of duty ended. He also told her Alaska had the highest ratio of men to women than anywhere else in the United States. Online dating was popular here and a lot of the men actually solicited mail-order brides.

After resting up at the hotel for a couple of hours, another limo had arrived to deliver them to the Outlaw Estates. Bailey couldn't help but chuckle when she remembered the marker at the entrance of the huge gated residence. It said, "Unless you're an outlaw, stay out. Josey Wales welcomed." Walker had told her the sign had been Maverick Westmoreland's idea. He was a huge fan of Clint Eastwood. The Outlaw mansion sat on over fifty acres of land.

Already Bailey had met Charm and Garth's brothers—Jess, Sloan, Cash and Maverick. In addition to their resemblance to the Westmorelands, they carried themselves like Westmorelands, as well. All five were single and, according to Charm, the thought of getting married made her brothers break out in hives. Jess, an attorney, seemed like the least rowdy of the four, and she wasn't surprised that he had announced his candidacy for senator of Alaska. He indicated he knew of Senator Reggie Westmoreland and although they hadn't met yet, Jess had been surprised to discover they were related. He looked forward to meeting Reggie personally. He'd been following Reggie's political career for a number of years and admired how he carried himself in Washington. He also knew of Chloe's father, Senator Jamison Burton, and hoped as many others did that he would consider running for president one day.

"Every Outlaw is here and accounted for except Dad. He's not dealing with all this very well and decided to make himself scarce tonight."

Garth cleared his throat, making it apparent that he felt

Charm had said too much. Bailey hadn't been bothered by Charm's words since on the flight over Walker had prepared her for the fact that Bart Outlaw still hadn't come around. For the life of her she couldn't understand what the big deal was. Why did Bart Outlaw refuse to acknowledge or accept that his father had been adopted?

Walker had also shared that Garth, his brothers and Charm all had different mothers but the brothers had been adopted by Bart before their second birthdays. Charm hadn't joined the group until she was in her teens. Her mother had sent her to Bart after Charm became too unruly. It sounded as if Bailey and Charm had a lot in common, although Dillon never entertained the thought of sending her anywhere.

One thing Bailey noted was that Walker never left her side. Not that it bothered her, but his solicitous manner made it obvious the two of them were more than friends. Every so often he would ask if she was okay. He'd told her before they'd arrived that if the Outlaws got too overbearing at any time, she and Walker would return to the hotel.

She saw a different Walker around the Outlaws. She knew he and Garth were best friends but it was obvious he had a close relationship with the others, as well. This Walker was more outgoing and not as reserved. But then he'd acted the same way around her brothers and cousins once he'd gotten to know them.

"How long are you staying in Fairbanks, Bailey?" Charm asked her. "I'm hoping you'll be here for a few days so we can get some shopping in."

Before she could answer, Walker spoke up. "Sorry to disappoint you, Charm, but Bailey's returning to Denver on Monday."

"Oh," Charm said, clearly disappointed.

Bailey didn't say anything, merely took a sip of her wine. It sounded as if Walker was counting the days.

"Well, I guess I'll have to make sure I'm included in that trip to Denver with my brothers later this month."

"Then, you'll be in luck because the women who married into the family, as well as me and my sister Megan, all love to shop," Bailey said, trying to put Walker's words to the back of her mind.

Charm's face broke into an elated grin.

Garth shook his head. "Shopping should be Charm's middle name." He checked his watch. "I hate to break up this conversation, but I think dinner is ready to be served."

Charm hooked Bailey's arm in hers as they headed toward the dining room and whispered, "So tell me, Bailey. Are there any real cute single guys in Denver?"

Walker sat with a tight jaw while he listened to Garth give his father hell. Deservedly so. Although Bart had finally shown up for dinner, he'd practically ignored Bailey. It had been obvious from his expression when he'd walked into the dining room and saw Bailey sitting beside Charm that he'd done a double take. He'd definitely noticed the resemblance between the two women. Yet that seemed to spike his resentment. So, like Garth and his brothers, Walker couldn't help wondering why Bart was so dead set against claiming the Westmorelands as kin. It seemed Garth was determined to find out.

After dinner, even before dessert could be served, Garth had encouraged Charm to show Bailey around while he and his brothers had quickly ushered their father upstairs. Garth had invited Walker to sit in on the proceedings.

"You were outright rude to Bailey, Dad."

Bart frowned. "I didn't invite her here."

"No, we did. And with good reason. She's our cousin."

"No, she's not. We are Outlaws, not Westmorelands."

"You're not blind, Dad. You saw the resemblance between Charm and Bailey with your own eyes. Bailey even remarked on how much you favor her father and uncle."

"That means nothing to me," Bart said stubbornly.

Garth drew in a deep breath, and Walker knew his best friend well enough to know he was getting fed up with his father's refusal to accept the obvious. "Why? Why are you so hostile to the idea that your father was adopted? That does not mean he wasn't an Outlaw. All it means is that he had other family—his biological family—that we can get to know. Why do you want to deprive us of that?"

A brooding Bart was silent as he glanced around the room at his sons and at Walker. It was Walker who received the most intense glare. "You were to take care of this, Walker. Things should not have gotten this far. You were to find a way to discredit them."

"That's enough, Dad! How could you even ask something like that of Walker?" Garth asked angrily.

Instead of answering, Bart jerked to his feet and stormed out of the room.

His sons watched his departure with a mixture of anger and confusion on their faces.

"What the hell is wrong with him?" Jess asked the others.

Garth shook his head sadly. "I honestly don't know. You weren't there that day Hugh first told us about the Westmorelands. Dad was adamant that we not claim them as relatives no matter what. When he found out I sent Walker anyway, he was furious."

Sloan shook his head. "There has to be a reason he is handling things this way."

"I agree," Maverick said, standing. "Something isn't right here."

"I agree with Maverick," Walker said. There was something about Bart's refusal to accept that his father was adopted that didn't make sense. "There has to be a reason

Bart is in denial. He might have his ways, but I've never figured him to be an irrational man."

"I agree," Cash said, shaking his head. "And he actually told you to find a way to discredit the Westmorelands?"

Walker nodded slowly. "You heard him for yourself."

"Damn," Sloan said, refilling his glass with his favorite after dinner drink. "I agree with Maverick and Walker. Something isn't right. Since Dad won't level with us and tell us what's going on, I suggest we hire someone to find out."

Cash glanced over at his brother, frowning. "Find out what?"

"Hell, I don't know" was Sloan's frustrated reply.

The room got quiet until Walker said, "Have any of you considered the possibility that there's something that went on years ago within the Outlaw family that you don't know about? Something that makes Bart feel he has to maintain that his father was the blood son of an Outlaw?"

Garth sat down with his drink. "I have to admit that thought has occurred to me."

"In that case," Jess said, "we need to find out what."

"You worried it might cause a scandal that will affect your campaign?" Sloan asked his brother.

"I have no idea," Jess said soberly. "But if there's something I need to worry about, then I want to find out before the media does."

Garth nodded. "Then, we're all in agreement. We look into things further."

Everyone in the room nodded.

"I'm sorry about my father's behavior at dinner, Bailey. I honestly don't know what has gotten into him," Charm said apologetically as she led Bailey back to the center of the house.

"No apology needed," Bailey said. "I was anticipating

such an attitude. Walker prepared me on the flight here from Kodiak. He said Bart might not be friendly to me."

"Um," Charm said, smiling. "Speaking of Walker. The two of you look good together. I'm glad he's finally gotten over his wife."

Bailey drew in a deep breath, not sure that was the case. It was quite obvious to her that he was still grieving the loss of his wife and son. And because of the magnitude of that grief, he refused to open up his heart to anyone else. "Looks can be deceiving, Charm."

She raised a brow. "Does that mean you're actually leaving to return to Denver on Monday?"

"No reason for me to stay. Like I said, looks can be deceiving."

Charm lifted her chin. "In this case, I think not. I've noticed the way Walker looks at you. He looks at you—"

Probably like a horny man, Bailey thought silently. There was no need to explain to Charm that the only thing between her and Walker was their enjoyment of sex with each other.

At that moment, Bailey's cell phone went off. At any other time she would have ignored it, wishing she'd remembered to turn off the ringer, but not this time. This particular ringtone indicated the call was from her cousin Bane.

"Forgive my rudeness," Bailey said to Charm as she quickly got the phone out of her purse, clicked it on and said to the caller, "Hold on a minute."

She then looked at Charm. "Sorry, but I need to take this call. It's my cousin Bane. He's a navy SEAL somewhere on assignment, and there's no telling when he'll have a chance to call me again."

"I understand. And if you need to talk privately you can use any of the rooms off the hall here. I'll be waiting for you downstairs in the main room."

Bailey gave Charm an appreciative smile. "Thanks." She quickly stepped inside one of the rooms and turned on the lights. "Bane? What's going on? Where are you?"

"Can't say. And I can't talk long. But I'm going to need your help."

"My help? For what?"

"I need to find Crystal."

Bailey frowned thoughtfully. "Bane, you know what Dillon asked you to do."

"Yes, Bay. Dil asked that I grow up and accept responsibility for my actions, to make something of myself before thinking about reclaiming Crystal. I promised him that I would and I have. Enough time has passed and I don't intend to wait any longer. In a couple of weeks I'll be on an extended military leave."

"An extended leave? Bane, are you okay?"

"I'll be better after I find Crystal, and I need your help, Bay."

Everyone had left the family room to return to the dining room for dessert except for Garth and Walker. Garth refilled Walker's glass with Scotch before proceeding to fill his own.

"So," Garth said, after taking a sip. "Do you think there's something Dad's not telling us?"

Walker, with his legs stretched out in front of him, sat back on the sofa and looked at Garth before taking a sip of his own drink. "Don't you?"

"Yes, and I'm going to hire a private detective. I don't want Hugh involved. He and Dad go way back, and there might be some loyalty there that I don't want to deal with."

"I agree. What about Regan? Isn't some member of her family a PI?"

Garth nodded, studying the drink in his glass. "Yes, her sister's husband. I met him once. He's an okay guy.

I understand he's good at what he does. I might call him tomorrow."

"I think that's a good idea."

They were silent for a spell and then Garth asked, "So what's going on with you and Bailey?"

Walker took another sip of his drink. "What makes you think something is going on?"

Garth rolled his eyes. "I can see, Walker."

Walker met his best friend's stare. "All you see is me interested in a woman who's hot. That's nice to have on those cold nights, especially for a man who's been without a female in his bed for a while. You heard her. She's leaving on Monday. Good riddance."

Bailey paused outside the closed door, not wanting to believe what Walker had just said. She'd been making her way back downstairs when she'd heard voices from one of the rooms. The voices belonged to Garth and Walker and when she'd heard her name she'd stopped.

Backing away from the door now, tears filled her eyes. She quickly turned and bumped right into Charm.

"Bailey, I was downstairs wondering if you'd gotten lost or something and—"

Charm stopped talking when she saw the tears in Bailey's eyes. "Bailey? What's wrong? Are you all right?"

Bailey swiped at her tears. "Yes, I'm fine."

Charm frowned. "No, you're not." She then glanced beyond Bailey to the closed door and the voices she heard. "What's going on? What did you hear? Did someone say something to upset you? Is Dad in that room with Garth and Walker? Did you overhear something Dad said?"

When Bailey didn't say anything, an angry Charm moved past her toward the door, ready to confront whoever was in the room about upsetting Bailey.

Bailey grabbed her hand. "No, please. Don't. It's okay."

She swiped again at her eyes. "Thanks for your family's hospitality, Charm, but I need to leave." Bailey wanted to put as much distance between her and Walker as she could. "Will you call me a cab? I need a ride to the airport."

Charm frowned. "The airport? What about Walker? What am I supposed to tell him?"

To go to hell, Bailey thought. But instead she said, "You can tell him I got a call...from a family member...and I need to get back to Denver immediately."

Charm's frown deepened. "Do you really want me to tell him that?"

"Yes."

Charm didn't say anything for a minute, then nodded. "Okay, but I won't call you a cab. I'll take you to the airport myself."

Garth stared hard at Walker. "What you just said is nothing more than bull and you know it."

Walker took another sip of his drink before quirking a brow. "Is it?"

"Yes. You've fallen in love with Bailey, Walker. Admit it."

Walker didn't say anything for a long minute. Garth knew him well. "Doesn't matter if you think it's bull or not."

"It does matter. When are you going to let go of the past, Walker? When are you going to consider that perhaps Bailey is your future?"

Walker shook his head. "No, she's not my future. She has these rules, you see. And one of them is that she will never leave Westmoreland Country. And I, on the other hand, made a deathbed promise to my father never to leave Hemlock Row again."

"But you will admit that you love her?" Garth asked.

Walker closed his eyes as if in pain. "Yes, I love her.

I love her so damn much. God knows I tried to fight it, but I couldn't. These past three weeks have been the best I've ever had. I thought I could live my life as a bitter and lonely man, but she's made me want more, Garth. She's made my house a real home. And she likes Hemlock Row."

"Then, what's the problem?"

He met Garth's inquisitive stare. "The problem is that I can't compete with her family. She needs them more than she could ever need me."

"Are you sure of that?"

"Yes. She's been homesick. I honestly didn't expect her to stay in Alaska this long. Already she's broken one of her rules."

"Maybe she had a reason to do so, Walker. Maybe you're that reason."

"I doubt it."

Garth was about to say something else when there was a knock on the door. "Come in."

Sloan entered. "Charm just left with Bailey."

Walker raised a brow. "Left? Where did they go? Don't tell me Charm talked Bailey into hitting some shopping mall tonight."

Sloan shook his head. "No. It seems Bailey got a call from some family member and had to leave. I don't know all the details but Charm is taking her to the airport. Bailey is booking a flight back to Denver. Tonight."

Sixteen

"Ma'am, please buckle your seat belt. The plane will be taking off in a minute."

Bailey nodded and did what the flight attendant instructed. She'd arrived at the Fairbanks airport with no luggage, just the clothes on her back. Charm had promised to go to the hotel and pack up her things and ship them to her. She would do the same for the clothes Bailey had left behind at Hemlock Row.

Luckily Bailey could change her ticket for a fee. And she didn't care that she had two connecting flights before she reached Denver, one in Seattle and the other in Salt Lake City. All she cared about was that in twelve hours she would be back in Westmoreland Country. She hadn't even called her family to let them know her change in plans. She would get a rental car at the airport and go straight to Gemma's house. She needed to be alone for a while before dealing with her family and their questions.

She drew in a deep breath, not wanting to think about

Walker. But all she could remember were the words he'd told Garth. So he would be glad when she was gone, would he? Well, he was getting his wish. She had been a fool to think he was worthy of her love. All he'd thought was that she was a hot body to sleep with.

But then, hadn't he told her up front all he wanted from her was a meaningless affair? Well, tonight he'd proved that what they'd shared had been as meaningless as it could get. Knowing it would take at least two hours before the plane landed in Seattle, she closed her eyes to soothe her tattered mind. At that moment she hoped she never saw Walker again.

"Damn her," Walker growled, taking his clothes out of the drawers and slinging them into the luggage that was opened on his bed. He intended to fly back to Kodiak Island tonight. There was no need to hang around. Bailey was why he'd left Hemlock Row to come here in the first place. And then what did she do? She hauled ass the first time she got a call from home.

However, now he knew that even that was a lie. Thinking she'd had a real family emergency, he'd placed a call to Dillon, who didn't know what he was talking about. As far as Dillon knew, nobody had called Bailey.

So now, on top of everything else, she had lied to him. She couldn't wait until Monday to leave? She had to leave tonight? Hell, she hadn't even taken the time to pack her clothes. What the hell was he supposed to do with them?

But what hurt more than anything was that she hadn't even had the decency to tell him goodbye. He felt like throwing something. Why did falling in love always end in heartache for him?

He continued to throw everything in his luggage when he heard a knock on the door. He hoped it wasn't Garth, trying to talk him out of leaving. There was no way he could stay. He wanted to go home to Hemlock Row, where loneliness was expected. Where he could drown his sorrows in a good stiff drink.

When the knocking continued, he moved to the door and snatched it open. Both Garth and Charm stood there. "I'm leaving tonight, Garth, and there's nothing you can say to stop me."

Garth and Charm walked past him to enter the hotel room. "I agree you should leave tonight, but not for Hemlock Row."

Walker looked at Garth. What he'd said didn't make any sense. "Then, where the hell am I supposed to go?"

"To head off Bailey. Stop her from making it to Denver."

That statement came from Charm. He glared at her. "And why on earth would I do that?"

Charm placed her hand on her hip and glared back at him. "Because you and Garth are the reason she left. I don't know what the two of you said about her while huddled in that room together tonight, but whatever you said, she overheard it and it had her in tears. I thought Dad was in there with you and figured he'd said something rude and gave him hell about it. But he said what Bailey overheard must have been a conversation between the two of you," she said, shifting her furious gaze between him and Garth.

Walker frowned. "For your information, I didn't say a damn thing that would have…"

He stopped speaking, swallowed hard and then glanced over at Garth. "Surely you don't think she heard—"

"All that crap you said?" Garth interrupted to ask, shaking his head. "I hope not. But what if she did?"

Walker rubbed a hand down his face. *Yes, what if she did?* "Damn it, I didn't mean it. In fact, later on in the conversation I admitted to falling in love with her."

"You love her?" Charm asked, smiling.

"Yes."

"Well, I doubt she heard that part. In fact, I'm one hundred percent certain she didn't. She was crying as if her heart was broken."

Walker checked his watch. "I've got to go after her."

"Yes, you do," Garth agreed. He then looked at Charm. "Do you have her flight information? I'm sure she has a connecting flight somewhere."

"She has two," Charm answered. "The first is in Seattle and then another in Salt Lake City."

Garth checked his watch. "I'll contact Regan and have her get the jet ready. If we act fast, you can get to Seattle the same time Bailey does. Maybe a few minutes before. And in case you've forgotten, Ollie is director of Seattle's Transportation Security Administration. Knowing the top dog of the TSA might prove to be helpful."

Walker nodded. He, Garth and Oliver Linton had served in the marines together and the three had remained good friends. "You're right." Walker was already moving, grabbing his coat and hat. Like Bailey, he was about to fly with just the clothes on his back.

Bailey took a sip of her coffee. She hated layovers, especially lengthy ones. She had another hour before she could board her connecting flight to Salt Lake City. And then she would have to wait two more hours before finally boarding the plane that would take her home to Denver.

Home.

Why didn't she have that excited flutter in her stomach that she usually had whenever she went on a trip and was on her way back to Denver? Why did she feel only hurt and pain? "That's easy enough to answer," she muttered to herself. "The man you love doesn't love you back. Get over it."

She drew in a deep breath, wondering if she ever would get over it. If it had been Monday and she'd been leaving because her time in Kodiak was over, it probably would have been different. But hearing the words Walker had spoken to Garth had cut deep. Not just into her heart but also into her soul. Evidently, her time at Hemlock Row had meant more to her than it had to him. All she'd been to him was a piece of ass during the cold nights. He'd practically said as much to Garth.

After finishing off her coffee, she tightened her coat around herself. For some reason she was still feeling the harsh Alaskan temperatures. She hated admitting it, but she missed Hemlock Row already, although she refused to miss Walker. She wished she could think of his ranch without thinking of him. She would miss Willie, Marcus and the guys, as well as Ms. Albright. She would miss standing at Walker's bedroom window every morning to stare out at Shelikof Strait. And she would definitely miss cooking in his kitchen. When she finally got around to designing her own home on Bailey's Bay, she might steal a few of his kitchen ideas. It would serve him right if she did.

"Excuse me, miss."

She glanced up into the face of an older gentleman wearing a TSA uniform. "Yes?"

"Are you Bailey Westmoreland?"

"Yes, I'm Bailey Westmoreland." She hoped nothing was wrong with her connecting flight. She didn't want the man to tell her it was canceled or delayed. She was ready to put as much distance between herself and Alaska as she could.

He nodded. "Ms. Westmoreland, could you please come with me?"

She stood. "Yes, but why? Is something wrong? What's going on?" She didn't have any luggage so there was no way they could have found anything in it. And her ticket was legit. She had made the proper changes in Fairbanks. As far as she was concerned she was all set.

"I'm unable to answer that. I was advised by my director to bring you to his office."

"Your director?" She swallowed. This sounded serious. She hoped she and some terrorist didn't have the same name or something. *Oh, crap.* "Look, sir," she said, following the man. "There must be some mistake."

She was about to say she'd never had done a bad thing in her life and then snapped her mouth shut. What about all those horrific things she, Bane and the twins had done while growing up? But that had been years ago. The sheriff of Denver, who was a good friend of Dillon's, had assured him that since the four of them had been juveniles their records would be wiped clean, as long as they didn't get into any trouble as adults. She couldn't speak for the twins, and Lord knew she couldn't vouch for Bane, but she could certainly speak for herself.

So she did. "Like I said, there must be a mistake. I am a law-abiding citizen. I work for a well-known magazine. I do own a gun. Several. But I don't have any of them with me."

The man stopped walking and looked over at her with a keen eye. She swallowed, wishing she hadn't said that. "I hunt," she quickly added, not wanting him to get the wrong idea. "I have all the proper permits and licenses."

He merely nodded. He then opened a door. "You can wait in here. It won't be long."

She frowned, about to tell him she didn't want to wait in there, that she was an American with rights. But she was too tired to argue. Too hurt and broken. She would wait for the director and see why she was being detained. If she needed an attorney there were a number of them in the Westmoreland family.

"Fine. I'll wait," she said, entering the room and glancing around. It was definitely warmer in here than it had been at the terminal gate. It was obvious this was some kind of meeting room, she thought, shrugging out of her coat and tossing it across the back of a chair. There were no windows, just a desk, several chairs and a garbage can. A map of Washington State was on one wall and a map of the United States on the other. There was a coffeepot on the table in the corner, and although she'd had enough coffee tonight to last her a lifetime, she crossed to the pot, hoping it was fresh.

That was when she heard the door behind her open. Good, the director had arrived and they could get down to business. The last thing she needed was to miss her connecting flight. She turned to ask the man or woman why she was here and her mouth dropped open.

The man who walked into the room was not the TSA director. It was the last person she figured she would see tonight or ever again.

"Walker!"

Seventeen

Walker entered the room and closed the door behind him. And then he locked it. Across the room stood the woman he loved more than life itself. She'd overheard things straight from his lips that had all been lies, and now he had to convince her he hadn't meant any of what he'd said.

"Hello, Bailey."

She backed up, shock written all over her face. "Walker, what are you doing here? How did you get here? *Why* are you here?"

He shoved his hands into his pockets. He heard the anger in her voice. He also heard the hurt and regretted more than ever what he'd said. "I thought we had a conversation once about you asking a lot of questions. But since I owe you answers to each and every one of them, here goes. I came here to talk to you. I got here with Garth's company jet. And I'm here because I owe you an apology."

She stiffened her spine. "You should not have bothered.

I don't think there's anything you can do or say to make me accept your apology."

He recalled when he'd said something similar to her the day she'd shown up at Hemlock Row. "But I did bother, because I know you heard what I said to Garth."

She crossed her arms over her chest. "Yes, I heard you. Pretty loud and clear. And I understood just what I was to you while I was at Hemlock Row and how you couldn't wait for me to leave."

"I didn't mean what I said."

"Sure you did. If nothing else, I've discovered you're a man who says exactly what he means."

He leaned against the wall, tilted his hat back and inhaled deeply, wishing her scent didn't get to him. And he wished she didn't look so desirable. She was still wearing the outfit she'd worn at the Outlaws'—black slacks and a bronze-colored pullover knit sweater with matching jewelry. She looked good then and she looked good now, four hours and over two thousand miles later.

But he liked Bailey best when she wasn't wearing anything at all. When she lay in his bed naked, with her breasts full and perky, the nipples wet from his tongue, and her feminine mound, hot, moist and ready for—

He sucked in a sharp breath and abruptly put an end to those thoughts. "Can we sit and talk?"

She frowned. "I honestly don't want to hear anything you have to say."

"Please. Both times when you apologized to me, I accepted your apologies."

"Good for you, but I have no intention of accepting yours."

She was being difficult, he knew that. He also knew there was only one way to handle Bailey. And that was by not letting her think she had the upper hand. "We are going to talk whether you want to listen to what I say or not. I locked that door," he said, removing his hat to place on a rack and then crossing the room to sit in one of the chairs. "And I don't intend for it to be opened until I say so. I forgot to mention that the director of the TSA here is an old marine friend of mine."

She glared at him. "You can't hold me here like some kind of hostage. I will sue you both."

"Go ahead and do that, if you desire. In the meantime you and I are staying in here until you agree to listen to what I have to say."

"I won't listen."

"I have the time to wait for you to change your mind," he said, leaning back in the chair so the front legs lifted off the floor. He closed his eyes. He heard her cross the room to the door and try it. It was locked. He didn't reopen his eyes when he heard her banging on it, nor when he heard her kick it a few times.

He knew the exact moment when a frustrated and angry Bailey crossed the room to stand in front of him. "Wake up, you bastard. Wake up and let me out of here."

He ignored her, but it wasn't easy. Especially when she began using profanity the likes of which he'd never heard before. He'd heard from one of her cousins that she used to curse like a sailor—worse than a sailor—as a teen, and Walker had even heard her utter a few choice words that day in his bedroom when he'd pissed her off. But now, tonight, she was definitely on a roll.

He would let her have her say—no matter how vulgar it was—and then he would have his. He would tell her everything. Including the fact that he loved her. He didn't expect her to love him back. It was too late for that, although he doubted it would have happened anyway. Bailey loved Westmoreland Country. She was married to it.

It seemed her filthy mouth wouldn't run out of steam anytime soon, so he decided to put an end to it. He'd gotten the picture, heard loud and clear what she thought of him. He slowly opened his eyes and stared at her. "If you recall, Bailey, I once told you that you had too delicious a mouth to fill it with nasty words. Do I need to test it to make sure it's still as delicious as the last time I tasted it?"

She threw her hair over her shoulder, fiery mad. "I'd like to see you try."

"Okay." He grabbed her around the waist and tumbled her into his lap. And then he kissed her.

She tried pushing him away, but just for a minute. Then, as if she had no control of her own tongue, it began tangling with his, sucking as hard as he was. And then suddenly, as if she realized what she was doing, she snatched her mouth away, but she didn't try getting off his lap.

"I hate you, Walker."

He nodded. "And I love you, Bailey."

She'd opened her mouth, probably to spew more filthy words, but what he'd said had her mouth snapping closed. She stared at him, not saying anything, and then she frowned. "I heard what you told Garth."

"Yes, but if you had hung around, you would have heard him say that I was talking bull because he knew how I felt about you. He's been my friend long enough to know. And then I admitted to having fallen in love with you."

She stared at him, studying his face. How long would it be before she said something? Finally she did. "You can't love me."

He shifted her in his lap, both to keep her there but also to bring some relief to the erection pressing painfully against his zipper. "And why can't I love you?"

"Because you're still in love with your wife. You've been grieving for her for ten years and you want me to believe I came along and changed that in less than a month?"

He knew he had to tell her the truth. All of it. He had to tell her what only he and Garth knew. Doing so would bring back memories. Painful memories. But he loved her. And he owed her the truth.

"Yes, I guess that would be hard to believe if I had been grieving for Kalyn for ten years. But I stopped loving my wife months before she died. I stopped loving her when I found out she was having an affair with another man."

Bailey swallowed. Of all the things she'd expected him to say, that wasn't it. "Your wife was unfaithful?" she asked, making sure she'd heard him correctly.

"Yes, among a number of other things."

She lifted a brow. "What other things?"

Walker drew in a deep breath before lifting her from his lap to place her in the chair beside him. He paced the room a few times before finally leaning against the wall.

"I need to start at the beginning," he said in a low, husky tone. But she'd been around Walker enough to detect the deep pain in his voice. "I was in the marines, stationed at Camp Pendleton. A few of the guys and I took a holiday to LA, preferring to tour the countryside. We came across a film crew making a movie. Intrigued, we stopped and, believe it or not, they asked us to be extras."

He paused before continuing, "One of the women who had a small role caught my eye and I caught hers."

"Kalyn?"

He looked over at Bailey. "Yes. That night she and I met at a restaurant and she told me her dream was to become an actress, that she was born in Los Angeles and loved the area. We slept together that night and a few times after that. I was smitten, but I thought that would be the end of it. It was only a few months before my time in the marines ended and I was looking forward to heading home. Both Garth and I were."

He paused. "Dad had written and I knew the ranch was

becoming a handful. He couldn't wait for me to come home to help. I told him I would. Practically promised."

He moved away from the wall to sit in the chair beside her. "I basically broke that promise. A few days before I was supposed to leave I got a call. Someone had viewed a clip of me as an extra and liked what they saw. They didn't know whether I could act or not but thought I had what they termed 'Hollywood looks.' They called me to try out for a part in some movie. I didn't get the part but they asked me to hang around for a week or two, certain they could find me work."

He leaned back in the chair as he continued. "Kalyn said she was happy for me. She also told me she thought she was pregnant. I never questioned her about it, although Garth suggested I should. I didn't listen to him. Nor did I listen when he tried to get me to leave California and return home, reminding me that my dad needed me. All I could think about was that Kalyn might be pregnant and I should do the honorable thing and marry her. So I did."

"Was she pregnant?" Bailey asked curiously.

"No. She said it was a false alarm, but I was determined to make my marriage work regardless. I loved her. I suggested we leave LA and move to Kodiak Island, but she wouldn't hear of it. She would cry every time I brought up the subject. She told me she hated a place she'd never seen and she never wanted to go there."

Bailey couldn't imagine anyone not liking Hemlock Row, especially before they'd seen it.

"I talked to my dad and he told me to stay with my wife and make my marriage work and that he would hire a couple more men to help out around the ranch," Walker continued. "Although he didn't say it, I knew he was disappointed that I wasn't coming home with my wife.

"A few months later I got the chance at a big role and my career took off from there. Kalyn was happy. She loved being in the spotlight as my wife. But I missed home and when I told her I'd made up my mind to leave and return to Alaska, she told me she was pregnant."

Bailey lifted a brow. "Was she really pregnant this time?" she asked in a skeptical voice. It sounded to her as though Kalyn's claim that first time had been a trick just to get Walker to marry her.

"Yes, she was this time. I went with her to the doctor to confirm it. Things got better between us. I fell in love with Connor the moment I heard his heartbeat. And months later, when I felt him move in Kalyn's stomach, I think my son and I connected in an unbreakable bond. I couldn't wait for him to be born. When he finally arrived I thought he was perfect. I couldn't wait to take him home for my parents to meet their grandson."

"You took him home to Hemlock Row?"

"Yes, but not until he was almost a year old. Kalyn refused to let me take him any sooner than that. Connor loved it there with his grandparents. I took him everywhere and showed him everything. Kalyn didn't go with us and told me I could only be gone with Connor for a week. I was upset about it but was grateful that my parents got to meet Connor and he got to meet them. A few months after I returned to LA I learned my mom was sick and the doctors couldn't figure out why. I went home a few times and each time I did, Kalyn gave me hell."

Bailey frowned. "She didn't want you to go home to check on your sick mother?" she asked, appalled.

"No, she didn't. Things got pretty bad between us, although we worked hard to pretend otherwise. In public we were the perfect, happily married Hollywood couple, but behind closed doors it was a different story."

He stood again to pace and when he came to a stop in front of where she sat, her heart almost stopped. The look on his face was full of hurt and anguish. "Then one day

I came home and she dropped a bombshell. She told me that for the past year and a half she'd been having an affair with a married man and he'd finally decided to leave his wife for her."

He drew in a deep breath and closed his eyes. When he reopened them, he said, "And she also wanted me to know that Connor was not my son."

"No!"

The pain of his words hit Bailey like a ton of bricks, so she could imagine how Kalyn's words must have hit him. The son he'd fallen in love with was not his biological son. She couldn't imagine the pain that must have caused him.

"I told her I didn't care if Connor was my biological son or not. He was the son of my heart and that's all that mattered. I loved him. She only laughed and called me a fool for loving a child that wasn't mine."

There were a lot of words Bailey could think of to describe Walker's deceased wife, and none of them were nice. "What happened after that? Did she move out?"

"No. Her lover must have changed his mind about leaving his wife. When I came home one evening after picking up Connor from day care, she ignored both of us and stayed in her room. I knew something was wrong, I just didn't know what.

"A few days later, on the set, I got a call letting me know there'd been an accident. It seemed Kalyn lost control of the car in the rain. She was killed immediately but Connor fought for his life. I rushed to the hospital in time to give my son blood. He'd lost a lot of it."

"So he *was* your biological son!"

"Yes, Connor was my biological son. She had intentionally lied to me, or she might have been sleeping with both me and her lover and honestly didn't know which one of us was Connor's father. Connor lasted another day and then I lost him. I lost my son."

A tear slipped from Bailey's eye, and when more tears began to fall, she swiped at them. He hadn't deserved what his wife put him through. No man would have deserved that.

"But that wasn't the worst of it," she heard him say as she continued swiping at her tears.

"It wasn't?" She couldn't imagine anything worse than that.

"No. After the funeral, I came home and found a letter Kalyn had written to me. She left it in a place where she figured I would find it."

Bailey's brows bunched. "A letter."

He nodded. "Yes. She wanted me to know the car wreck wasn't an accident. It was intentional."

Bailey's heart stopped. "Are you saying that…" She couldn't finish the question.

"Yes," he said softly with even deeper pain in his voice. "Kalyn committed suicide. Being rejected by her lover was too much for her and she couldn't live another day. She wanted to take her lover's son with her."

She saw the tears misting his eyes. No wonder his son was buried in his family's cemetery but his son's mother was not. The awful things she'd done, and the fact that she'd hated Hemlock Row sight unseen.

"Nobody knows about that letter but Garth. He was with me when I found it. We decided turning it over to the authorities would serve no purpose. It would be better to let everyone continue to believe what happened had been an accident."

Bailey nodded. "Did you ever find out the identity of Kalyn's lover?"

"No, although I had my suspicions. I never knew for certain." He paused. "I told myself that I would never love or trust another woman. And I hadn't. Until you. I didn't want to fall in love with you, Bailey. God knows I fought it tooth and nail. But I couldn't stop what was meant to be. Yes, I said what I said to Garth, but I was in denial, refusing to accept what I knew in my heart was true. I'm sorry for the words I said. But the truth is that I do love you. I love you more than I've ever loved any other woman."

She eased out of the chair and went to him, pulled him to her and held him. He had been through so much. He had lost so much. He had experienced the worst betrayal a man could suffer. Not only had Kalyn intentionally taken her life, she had taken the life of an innocent child.

Walker pulled back and looked at her. "I know there can never be anything between us. You don't love me and I understand that. You're in love with your land, and I accept that, too, because I'm in love with mine. I made Dad another promise, this one I intend to keep. I'll never leave Hemlock Row again."

She stared deep into the dark eyes that had always mesmerized her. "You just said you loved me, yet you're willing to let me go back to Westmoreland Country?"

"Yes, because that's your real love. I know your rules, Bailey."

A smile touched her lips. "And I'm breaking the one I thought I would never break."

He looked at her questionably. "What are you saying?"

She wrapped her arms around his neck. "I'm saying that I love you, too. I realized I loved you weeks ago. I think that's why I came to Kodiak to personally apologize. I missed you, although I would never have admitted that to myself or to you. I do love you, Walker, and more than anything I want to make a home with you at Hemlock Row."

"B-but what about Westmoreland Country?"

She chuckled. "I love my home, but Gemma and Megan were right. Home is where the heart is, and my heart is with you."

He studied her features intently. "Are you sure?"

She chuckled again. "I am positive. I'm officially breaking Bailey's Rules."

And then she slanted her mouth over his, knowing their lives together were just beginning.

A few days later, Walker eased out of the bed. Bailey grabbed his thigh. "And where do you think you're going?"

He smiled. "To stoke the fire. I'll be back."

"Holding you to it, Alaskan."

Walker chuckled. He couldn't believe how great his life was going. Everyone was happy that he'd gotten everything straightened out with Bailey and she had decided to stay. Next week was Thanksgiving and they would leave Kodiak Island to spend the holiday with her family in Westmoreland Country.

After stoking the fire and before he returned to bed, he went to the drawer and retrieved the package he'd put there earlier that day. Grabbing the box, he went back to the bed.

"Bailey?" She opened her eyes to look at him. "Yes?"

"Will you marry me?"

When she saw the box he held she almost knocked him over struggling to sit up. "You're proposing to me?"

He smiled. "Yes."

"B-but I'm in bed, naked and—"

"Just made love to me. I can't think of any other way to complete things. I want you to know it's never been just sex with us…although I think the sex is off the charts."

She grinned. "So do I."

He opened the box and she gasped at the ring shining back at her in the firelight. "It's beautiful, Walker."

"As beautiful as my future wife," he said, sliding the ring on her finger. Halfway there, he stopped and eyed her expectantly. "You didn't say yes."

"Yes!"

He slid the ring the rest of the way and then pulled her

into his arms. "My parents would have loved you," he whispered against her ear.

"And I would have loved them, too. And I would have loved Connor."

He pulled back. "He would have loved you." Walker held her hand up and looked at it. "I thought the timing was right since I'll be taking you home next week. I don't want your family to think I'm taking advantage of you. When they see that ring they will know. I love you and intend to make you my wife. Just set the date. But don't make me wait too long."

"I won't."

He brushed his thumb across her cheek. "Thanks for believing I was worthy of breaking your rules, Bailey."

"And thanks for believing I am worthy of your love and trust, Walker."

Their mouths touched, and she knew tonight was the beginning of how things would be for the rest of their lives.

Epilogue

Thanksgiving Day

Bailey looked around the huge table. This was the first time that every one of her brothers, sisters and cousins—the Denver Westmorelands—had managed to come home for Thanksgiving. Even Bane was here. The family had definitely multiplied with the addition of wives, husbands and children. She and Walker would tie the knot here in Westmoreland Country on Valentine's Day.

Everyone was glad to see Bane. It had been years since he'd been home for Thanksgiving. In fact, they hadn't seen him since that time he'd shown up unannounced at Blue Ridge Land Management, surprising Stern and Adrian.

Bailey wondered if she was the only one who noticed he seemed pensive and preoccupied. And not for the first time she wondered if something had happened on his last covert operation that he wasn't sharing with them.

"You okay, baby?" Walker leaned over to ask her.

She smiled at him. "Yes, I'm fine. You love me and I love you, so I couldn't be better."

The announcement that she was marrying and leaving Westmoreland Country had everyone shocked. But all they had to do was look at her and Walker to see how happy they were together.

Thanks to Lucia and Chloe, Bailey would still work for *Simply Irresistible*, working remotely from Kodiak Island. She'd been doing it for a while now and so far things were working out fine.

The Outlaws, all six of them, had come to visit, and just like Bailey had known, everyone had gotten along beautifully. They were invited to the Denver Westmorelands' annual foundation banquet and said they would return in December to attend. That way they would get to meet their Westmoreland cousins from Atlanta, Montana, North Carolina and Texas. Word was that Bart still hadn't come around. According to Walker, Garth intended to find out why his father was being so difficult.

Since Gemma, Callum and their kids were in town, Bailey and Walker were staying at the bed-and-breakfast inn Jason's wife, Bella, owned. It was perfect, and she and Walker had the entire place to themselves.

Bailey figured she would eventually get around to building her own place so she and Walker could have somewhere private whenever they came to visit, but she wasn't in any hurry.

After clinking on his glass to get everyone's attention, Dillon stood. "It's been years since we've had everyone together on Thanksgiving, and I'm thankful that this year Gemma and Bane were able to come home to join us. And I'm grateful for all the additions to our family, especially one in particular," he said, looking over at Walker and smiling.

"I think Mom, Dad, Uncle Thomas and Aunt Susan

would be proud of what we've become and that we're still a family."

Bailey wiped a tear from her eye. Yes, they were still a family and always would be. She reached under the table for Walker's hand. She had everything she could possibly want and more.

"You wanted to see me, Dil?" Bane asked, walking into Dillon's home office. Out the window was a beautiful view of Gemma Lake.

Dillon glanced up as his brother entered. Bane appeared taller, looked harder, more mature than he'd seemed the last time he'd been home. "Yes, come on in, Bane."

Dinner had ended a few hours ago and after a game of snow volleyball the ladies had gathered in the sitting room to watch a holiday movie with the kids, and the men had gathered upstairs for a card game. "I want to know how you're doing," Dillon said, studying his baby brother.

"Fine, although my last assignment took a toll on me. I lost a good friend."

Dillon shook his head sadly. "I'm sorry to hear that."

"Me, too. Laramie Tucker was a good guy. The best. We went through the academy together."

Dillon knew not to ask what happened. Bane had explained a while back that all his assignments were confidential. "Is that why you're taking a military leave?"

Bane eased down in the chair across from Dillon's desk. "No. It's time I find Crystal. If nothing else, Tuck's death taught me how fragile life is. You can be here today and gone tomorrow."

Dillon came around and sat on the edge of his desk to face his brother. "Not sure if you knew it, but Carl Newsome passed away a few years ago."

Bane shook his head. "No, I didn't know."

"So you haven't seen Crystal since the Newsomes sent her away?"

"No. You were right. I didn't have anything to offer her at the time. I was a hothead and Trouble was my middle name. She deserved better, and I was willing to make something of myself to give her better."

Dillon nodded. "It's been years, Bane. The last time I talked to Emily Newsome was when I heard Carl had died. I called to offer my condolences. I asked about Crystal and Emily said Crystal was doing fine. She was working on her master's degree at Harvard with plans to get a doctorate."

Bane didn't say anything as he listened to what Dillon was saying. "That doesn't surprise me. Crystal was always smart in school."

Dillon stared at his brother, wondering how Bane had figured that out when most of the time he and Crystal were playing hooky. "I don't want to upset you, Bane. But you don't know what Crystal's feelings are for you. The two of you were teens back then. First love doesn't always mean last love. Although you might still love her, for all you know, she might have moved on. Have you ever considered the possibility that she might be involved with someone else?"

Bane leaned back in his chair. "I don't believe that. Crystal and I had an understanding. We have an unbreakable bond."

"But that was years ago. You just said you haven't seen her since that day Carl sent her away. For all you know, she could be married by now."

Bane shook his head. "Crystal wouldn't marry anyone else."

Dillon lifted a brow. "And how can you be so sure of that?"

Bane held his brother's stare. "Because she's already married, Dil. Crystal is married to me, and I think it's time to go claim my wife."

* * * * *

Don't miss the final Westmoreland hero!
BANE
Available December 2015,
only from New York Times *bestselling author*
Brenda Jackson
and Harlequin Desire!

If you loved Bailey's story,
pick up the very first Westmoreland novels,
now available in a convenient box set!

Volume One
Brenda Jackson's THE WESTMORELANDS
Books One to Five

DELANEY'S DESERT SHEIKH
A LITTLE DARE
THORN'S CHALLENGE
STONE COLD SURRENDER
RIDING THE STORM

If you're on Twitter, tell us what you think
of Harlequin Desire! #harlequindesire

RECLAIMED BY
THE RANCHER
Janice Maynard

One

Not much rattled Jeff Hartley. At twenty-nine, he owned and operated the family ranch where he had grown up during a near-idyllic childhood. His parents had taken early retirement back in the spring and had headed off to a condo on Galveston Bay, leaving their only son to carry on the tradition.

Jeff was a full member of the prestigious Texas Cattleman's Club, a venerable establishment where the movers and shakers of Royal, Texas, met to shoot the breeze and oftentimes conduct business. Jeff prided himself on being mature, efficient, easygoing and practical.

But when he opened his door on a warm October afternoon and saw Lucy Peyton standing on his front porch, it felt as if a bull had kicked him in the chest. First there was the dearth of oxygen, a damned scary feeling. Then the pain set in. After that, he had the impulse to flee before the bull could take another shot.

He stared at his visitor, his gaze as level and dispassionate as he could make it. "I plan to vote Democrat this year. I don't need any magazine subscriptions. And I already have a church home," he said. "But thanks for stopping by."

He almost had the door closed before she spoke. "Jeff. Please. I need to talk to you."

Damn it. How could a woman say his name—one measly syllable—and make his insides go all wonky? Her voice was every bit the same as he remembered. Soft and husky…as if she were on the verge of laryngitis. Or perhaps about to offer some lucky man naughty, unspeakable pleasure in the bedroom.

The sound of eight words, no matter how urgently spoken, shouldn't have made him weak in the knees.

Her looks hadn't changed, either, though she was a bit thinner than he remembered. Her dark brown hair, all one length but parted on the side, brushed her shoulders. Hazel eyes still reminded him of an autumn pond filled with fallen leaves.

She was tall, at least five-eight…and though she was athletic and graceful, she had plenty of curves to add interest to the map. Some of those curves still kept him awake on dark, troubled nights.

"Unless you're here to apologize," he said, his words deliberately curt, "I don't think we have anything to talk about."

When she shoved her shoulder against the door, he had to step back or risk hurting her. Even so, he planted himself in the doorway, drawing a metaphorical line in the sand.

Her eyes widened, even as they flashed with temper. "How *dare* you try to play the wronged party, you *lying, cheating, sonofa*—"

Either she ran out of adjectives, or she suddenly realized that insulting a man was no way to gain entry into his home.

He lifted an eyebrow. "You were saying?"

His mild tone seemed to enrage her further, though to her credit, she managed to swallow whatever additional words trembled on her tongue. Was it bad of him to remember that small pink tongue wetting his— Oh, hell. Now *he* was the one who pulled up short. Nothing stood to be gained by indulging in a sentimental stroll down memory lane.

No tongues. No nothing.

She licked her lips and took a deep, visible breath. "Samson Oil is trying to buy the Peyton ranch."

Two

Lucy was diabetic; she'd been diagnosed as a twelve-year-old. If she didn't take her insulin, she sometimes got the shakes. But nothing like this. Facing the man she had come to see made her tremble from head to toe. And she couldn't seem to stop. No amount of medicine in the world was ever going to cure her fascination with the ornery, immoral, two-faced, spectacularly handsome Jeff Hartley.

At the moment, however, he was her only hope.

"May I come in?" she asked, trying not to notice the way he smelled of leather and lime and warm male skin.

Jeff stared at her long enough to make her think he might actually say no. In the end, however, gentlemanly manners won out. "Ten minutes," he said gruffly. "I have plans later."

If he meant to wound her, his barb was successful… though she would never give him the satisfaction of knowing for sure. As they navigated the few steps into his living room and sat down, she found herself swamped with memories. This old farmhouse dated back three generations. It had been lovingly cared for and well preserved.

For one brief second, everything came crashing back: the hours she had spent in this bright, cheerful home, the master bedroom upstairs with the queen-size mattress and double-wedding-ring quilt, the bed Jeff had complained was too small for his six-foot-two frame…

She didn't want to remember. Not at all. Not even the spot in this very room where Jeff Hartley had gone down on one knee and offered her a ring and his heart.

Dredging up reserves of audacity and courage, she ignored the past and cut to the chase. "My cousin is trying to sell his land to Samson Oil." Recently, the outsider company had begun buying up acreage in Royal, Texas, at an alarming rate.

Jeff sat back in a leather armchair and hitched one ankle across the opposite knee, drawing attention to his feet. "Is it a fair offer?"

Nobody Lucy had ever known wore scuffed, hand-tooled cowboy boots as well as Jeff Hartley. At one time she wondered if he slept in the damned things. But then came that memorable evening when he showed her how a woman could take off a man's boots at the end of the day…

Her face heated. She jerked her thoughts back to the present. "More than fair. But that's not the point. The property has been in the Peyton family for almost a century. The farmland has contributed to Maverick County's food supply for decades. Equally important—the wildlife preserve was my grandfather's baby. Samson Oil will ruin everything."

"Why does Kenny want to sell?"

"He's sick of farming. He swears there's nothing for him in Royal anymore. He's decided to move to LA and try for an acting career. He pointed out that I sold most of my share to him, left for college and then stayed away. He wants his chance. But he needs cash."

"And this is my problem, how?"

Three

Lucy bit her lip until she tasted blood in her mouth. She couldn't afford to let Jeff goad her into losing her temper. It had happened far too easily on his front porch a moment ago. Her only focus right now should be on getting what she needed to stop a bad, bad decision.

It might have helped if Jeff had gotten old and fat in the past two years. But unfortunately, he looked better than ever. Dark blond hair in need of a trim. Piercing green eyes, definitely on the hostile side. And a long, lean body and lazy gait that made grown women sigh with delight whenever he sauntered by.

"I need you to loan me twenty thousand dollars," she blurted out. "The farm is self-supporting, but Kenny doesn't have a lot of liquid assets. He may be bluffing. Even if he's serious, though, twenty grand will get him off my back and send him on his way. He thinks the only choice he has for coming up with relocation funds is to un-load the farm, but I'm trying to give him another option."

"What will happen to the farm when he goes to the West Coast?"

It was a good question. And one she had wrestled with ever since Kenny told her he wanted to leave town. "I suppose I'll have to come back to Royal and take over. At least until Kenny crashes and burns in California and decides to return home."

"You don't have much faith in him, do you?"

She shrugged. "Our fathers were brothers. So we share DNA. But Kenny has always had a problem with focus. Six months ago he wanted to go to vet school. Six months before that he was studying to take the LSAT."

"But you already have a career…right? As a physical trainer? In Austin? That fancy master's degree you earned in sports medicine won't do you much good out on the farm." He didn't even bother to hide the sarcasm.

She wanted to squirm, but she concentrated on breathing in and breathing out, relaxing her muscles one set at a time. "Fortunately, mine is the kind of job that's in demand. I'm sure they won't hold my exact position, but there will be plenty of similar spots when I go back."

"How long do you think you'll have to stay here in Royal?"

"A few months. A year at the most. Will you loan me the money, or not?"

Jeff scowled. "You've got a lot of balls coming to me for help, Lucy."

"You *owe* me," she said firmly. "And you know it." This man…this beautiful, rugged snake of a man had been responsible for the second worst day of her life.

He sat up and leaned forward, resting his elbows on his knees. His veneer of calm peeled away, leaving a male who was a little bit frightening. Dark emerald eyes judged her and found her wanting. "I don't *owe* you a single damn thing. You're the one who walked out on our wedding and made me a laughingstock in Royal."

She jumped to her feet, heart pounding. Lord, he made her mad. "Because I caught you at our rehearsal dinner kissing the maid of honor," she yelled.

Four

Something about Lucy's meltdown actually made Jeff feel a little bit better about this confrontation. At least she wasn't indifferent.

"Sit down, Lucy," he said firmly. "If money is going to change hands, I have two conditions."

She did sit, but the motion looked involuntary...as if her knees gave out. "Conditions?"

"It's a lot of money. And besides, why ask me? Me, of all people?"

"You're rich," she said bluntly, her stormy gaze daring him to disagree.

It was true. His bank account was healthy. And sadly, Lucy had no family to turn to, other than her cousin. Lucy's parents and Kenny's had been killed in a boating accident eight years ago. Because of that tragedy, Lucy had a closer relationship with her cousin than one might expect. They were more like siblings, really.

"If my bottom line is good, it's partly because I don't toss money out the window on a whim."

"It wouldn't be a whim, Jeff. I know the way you think. This thing with Samson Oil is surely eating away at you. *Outsiders*. Taking over land that represents the history of Royal. And then doing God knows what with it. Drilling for oil that isn't there. Selling off the dud acres. Shopping malls. Big box stores. Admit it. The thought makes you shudder. You have to be suspicious about why a mysterious oil company is suddenly trying to buy land that was checked for oil years ago."

That was the problem with old girlfriends. They knew a man's weaknesses. "You're not wrong," he said slowly, taken aback that she had pegged him so well. "But in that case, why wouldn't I buy Kenny's land outright? And make sure that it retains its original purpose?"

"Because it's not the honorable thing to do. Kenny will see the light one day soon. And he would be devastated to come back to Royal and have nothing. Besides, that would be a whole lot more money. Twenty thousand is chicken feed to you."

Jeff grimaced. "You must know some damn fine chickens."

Perhaps she understood him better than he wanted to admit, because after laying out her case, she sat quietly, giving him time to sort through the possibilities. Lucy stared at him with hazel eyes that reflected wariness and a hint of grief.

He felt the grief, too. Had wallowed in it for weeks. But a man had to move on with his life. At one time, he'd been absolutely sure he would grow old with this woman. Now he could barely look at her.

"I need to think about it," he said.

Lucy's temper fired again. "Since when do you have

trouble making decisions?" Her hands twisted together in her lap as if she wanted to wrap them around his neck.

"Don't push me, Lucy." He scowled at her. "I'll pick you up out at the farm at five. We'll have dinner, and I'll give you my answer."

Her throat worked. "I don't want to be seen with you."

Five

The barb wasn't unexpected, but it took Jeff's breath momentarily. "The feeling is mutual," he growled. "I'll make reservations in Midland. We'll discuss my terms."

"But that's fifty miles away."

Her visible dismay gave him deep masculine satisfaction. It was time for some payback. Lucy deserved to twist in the wind for what she had done to him. A man's pride was everything.

"Take it or leave it," he said, the words curt.

"I thought you had plans later."

"You let me worry about my calendar, sweetheart."

He watched her flinch at his overt sarcasm. For a moment, he was ashamed of baiting her. But he shored up his anger. Lucy deserved his antagonism and more.

The silence grew in length and breadth, thick with unspoken emotions. If he listened hard enough, he thought he might even be able to hear the rapid beat of her heart. Like a defenseless animal trapped in a cage of its own making.

"Lucy?" He lifted an eyebrow. "I don't have all day."

"You could write me a check this instant," she protested. "Why make me jump through hoops?"

"Maybe because I can."

He was being a bastard. He knew it. And by the look on Lucy's face, she knew it, as well. But the opportunity to make her bend to his will was irresistible.

The fact that each of them could still elicit strong emotions from the other should have been a red flag. But then again, that was the story of their relationship. Though he and Lucy had grown up in the same town, they hadn't really known each other. Not until she'd come home to Royal for a lengthy visit after college graduation.

Lucy's parents had been dead by then. Instead of bunking with her cousin Kenny, Lucy had stayed with her childhood friend and college roommate, Kirsten. One of Kirsten's friends had thrown a hello-to-summer bash, and that's where Jeff had met the luscious Lucy.

He still remembered the moment she'd walked into the room. It was a case of instant lust…at least on his part. She was exactly the kind of woman he liked…tall, confident, and with a wicked sense of humor. The two of them had found a private corner and flirted for three hours.

A week later, they'd ended up in bed together.

Unfortunately, their whirlwind courtship and speedy five-month trip to the altar had ended in disaster. Ironically, if they had followed through with their wedding, two days from now would have been their anniversary.

Did Lucy realize the bizarre coincidence?

She stood up and walked to the foyer. "I have to go." The words were tossed over her shoulder, as if she couldn't wait to get out of his house.

He shrugged and followed her, putting a hand high on the door to keep her from escaping. "I don't want to make a trip out to the farm for nothing. So don't try standing me up. If you want the money, you'll get it on my terms or not at all."

Six

Lucy hurried to her car, heartsick and panicked. Why had she ever thought she could appeal to Jeff Hartley's sense of right and wrong? The man was a scoundrel. She was so angry with herself…angry for approaching him in the first place, and even angrier that apparently she was still desperately in love with him…despite everything he had done.

During the past two years, she had firmly purged her emotional system of memories connected to Jeff Hartley. Never once did she think of the way his arms pulled her tight against his broad chest. Or the silkiness of his always rumpled hair. At night in bed, she surely didn't remember how wonderful it was to feel him slide on top of her and into her, their breath mingling in ragged gasps and groans of pleasure.

Stupid man. She parked haphazardly at the farm and went in search of her cousin. She found him in the barn repairing a harness.

Kenny looked up when she entered. "Hey, Luce. What's up?"

She plopped down on a bale of hay. "How much would it take for you not to sell the land?"

He frowned. "What do you mean? Are you trying to buy it for yourself?"

"Gosh, no. I'd be a terrible farmer. But I have a gut feeling you'll change your mind down the road. And I'm willing to keep things running while you sow your wild oats. So I'm asking…would twenty grand be enough to bankroll your move to LA and get you started? It would be a loan. You'd have to pay back half eventually, and I'll pay back the other half as a thank-you for not letting go of Peyton land."

The frown grew deeper. "A loan from whom?"

Kenny might pretend to be a goofball when it suited him, but the boy was smart…and he knew his grammar.

"From a friend of mine," she said. "No big deal."

Kenny perched on the bale of hay beside hers and put an arm around her shoulders. "What have you done, Luce?"

She sniffed, trying not to cry. "Made a deal with the devil?"

"Are you asking me or telling me?"

Kenny was two years younger than she was. Most of the time she felt like his mother. But for the moment, it was nice to have someone to lean on. "I think Jeff Hartley is going to loan it to me."

"Hell, no." Kenny jumped to his feet, raking both hands through his hair agitatedly. "The man cheated on you and broke your heart. I won't take his money. We'll think of something else. Or I'll convince you it's okay to sell the farm."

"You'll never convince me of that. What if being an actor doesn't pan out?"

"Do you realize how patronizing you sound, Luce? No

offense, but what I want to do is more serious than *sowing wild oats*."

She rubbed her temples with her fingertips. "I shouldn't have said that. I'm sorry."

After a few moments, he went back to repairing the harness. "Why did you go to Jeff, Lucy? Why him?"

Bowing her head, she let the tears fall. "The day after tomorrow would have been our wedding anniversary. Jeff Hartley still owes me for that."

Seven

Jeff made arrangements to have the Hartley Ranch covered, personnel wise, in the event that he didn't return from Midland right away. There was no reason in the world to think that he and Lucy might end up in bed together, but he was a planner. A former Boy Scout. Preparation was second nature to him.

As he went about his business, his mind raced on a far more intimate track. Lucy had betrayed the wedding vows she and Jeff had both written. Before they'd ever made it to the altar. And yet she thought Jeff was the one at fault. Even from the perspective of two years down the road, he was still angry about that.

At four o'clock, he showered and quickly packed a bag. He traveled often for cattle shows and other business-related trips, so he was accustomed to the drill. Then he went online and ordered a variety of items and had them delivered to his favorite hotel.

When he was satisfied that his plans were perfectly in

order, he loaded the car, stopped by the bank, and then drove out to the farm. There was at least a fifty-fifty chance Lucy would shut the door in his face. But he was convinced her request for a loan was legit. In order to get the cash, she had to go along with his wishes.

Unfortunately, Kenny answered the door. And he was spoiling for a fight.

Jeff had spent his entire life in Texas. He was no stranger to brawls and the occasional testosterone overload. But if he had plans for himself and Lucy, first he had to get past her gatekeeper. He held up his hands in the universal gesture for noncombative behavior. "I come in peace, big guy."

"Luce never should have asked you for the money. I can manage on my own."

"In LA? I don't think so. Not without liquidating your assets. And that will break your cousin's heart. Is that really what you want to do?"

"You're hardly the man to talk about breaking Lucy's heart." But it was said without heat. As if Kenny understood that more was at stake here than his would-be career.

"Where is she?" Jeff asked. "We need to go."

"I think she was on the phone, but she'll be out soon. Though I sure as hell don't know why."

"Lucy and I have some unfinished business from two years ago. It's time to settle a few scores."

Kenny blanched. "I don't want to be in the middle of this."

"Too late. You shouldn't have tried to sell your land to Samson Oil. And besides, Lucy came to me…not the other way around. What does that tell you?"

Kenny bristled. "It tells me that my cousin cares about me. I have no idea what it says about you."

Eight

Lucy stood just out of sight in the hallway and listened to the two men argue. Strangely, there was not much real anger in the exchange. At one time, Kenny and Jeff had been good friends. Kenny was supposed to walk Lucy down the aisle and hand her over to the rancher who had swept her off her feet. But that moment never happened.

Lucy cleared her throat and eased past Kenny to step onto the porch. "Don't worry if I'm late," she said.

Kenny tugged her wrist and leaned in to kiss her on the cheek. "Text me and let me know your plans. So I don't worry."

His droll attempt to play mother hen made her smile. "Very funny. But yes… I'll be in touch."

At last she had to face Jeff. He stood a few feet away, his expression inscrutable. In a dark tailored suit, with a crisp white dress shirt and blue patterned tie, he looked like a man in charge of his domain. A light breeze ruffled his hair.

His sharp, intimate gaze scanned her from head to toe. "Let's go" was all he said.

Lucy sighed inwardly. So much for her sexy black cocktail dress with spaghetti straps. The daring bodice showcased her cleavage nicely. Big surly rancher barely seemed to notice.

They descended the steps side by side, Jeff's hand on her elbow. He helped her into the car, closed her door and went around to slide into the driver's seat. The car was not one she remembered. But it had all the bells and whistles. It smelled of leather and even more faintly, the essence of the man himself.

For the first ten miles silence reigned. Pastures of cattle whizzed by outside the window, their existence so commonplace, Lucy couldn't pretend a deep interest in the scenery. Instead, she kicked off her shoes, curled her legs beneath her, and leaned forward to turn on the satellite radio.

"Do you mind?" she asked.

Jeff shot her a glance. "Does being alone with me make you nervous, Lucy?"

"Of course not." Her hand hovered over the knob. More than anything else, she wanted music to fill the awkward silence. But if Jeff saw that as a sign of weakness, then she wouldn't do it.

She sat back, biting her bottom lip. Now the silence was worse. Before, they had simply been two near strangers riding down the road. Jeff's deliberately provocative question set her nerves on edge.

"While we're on our way," she said, "why don't you tell me what these conditions are? The ones I have to agree to so you'll loan me the money?"

Jeff didn't answer her question. "I'm curious. Why doesn't Kenny go out and get his own loan?"

"He's shoveled everything he has back into the farm.

His credit's maxed out. Besides, his solution is selling to Samson Oil. I explained that."

"True. You did."

"So tell me, Jeff. What do you want from me?"

Nine

What do you want from me? Lucy's frustrated question was one Jeff would have been glad to answer. In detail. Slowly. All night. But first there were hurdles to jump.

Though he kept his hands on the wheel and his eyes on the road, he had already memorized every nuance of his companion's appearance. Everything from her sexy black high heels all the way up to her sleek and shiny hair tucked behind one ear.

Her black cocktail dress, at first glance, was entirely appropriate for dinner in the big city. But damned if he wasn't going to have the urge to take off his jacket and wrap her up in it. He didn't want other men looking at her.

He felt possessive, which was ridiculous, because Lucy was definitely her own woman. If she chose to prance stark naked down Main Street, he couldn't stop her. So maybe he needed to take a different tack entirely. Instead of bossing her around, perhaps he should use another very enjoyable means of communication.

Right now, she was a hen with ruffled feathers. He had upset her already. The truth was, he didn't care. He'd rather have anger from Lucy than outright indifference.

He could work with anger.

"We'll talk about the specifics over dinner, Lucy. Why don't you relax and tell me about your work in Austin."

His diversion worked for the next half hour. In his peripheral vision, he watched as Lucy's body language went from tense and guarded to normal. Or at least as normal as it could be given the history between them.

Later, when he pulled up in front of the luxury hotel in the heart of the city, Lucy shot him a sharp-eyed glance.

He took her elbow and led her inside. "The restaurant here is phenomenal," he said. "I think you'll enjoy it."

Over appetizers and drinks, Lucy thawed further. "So far, I'm impressed. I forgot to eat lunch today, so I was starving."

Jeff was hungry, too, but he barely tasted the food. He was gambling a hell of a lot on the outcome of this encounter.

They ordered the works…filet and lobster. With spinach salad and crusty rolls. Clearly, Lucy enjoyed her meal. *He* enjoyed the fact that she didn't fuss about calories and instead ate with enthusiasm.

Good food prepared from fresh ingredients was a sensual experience. It tapped into some of the same pleasure centers as lovemaking. It was hard to bicker under the influence of a really exceptional Chablis and a satisfying, special-occasion dinner.

That's what he was counting on…

Lucy declined dessert. Jeff did, as well. As they lingered over coffee, he could practically see her girding her loins for battle.

She stirred a single packet of sugar into her cup and sat back in her chair, eyeing him steadily. "Enough stalling,

Jeff. I've come here with you for dinner, which was amazing, I might add. But I need to have your answer. Will you loan me the money, and what are your conditions?"

Ten

Lucy was braced for bad news. It was entirely possible that Jeff had brought her here—wined and dined her—in order to let her down gently. To give her an outright no.

Watching him take a sip of coffee was only one of many mistakes she had made tonight. When his lips made contact with the rim of his thin china cup, she was almost sure the world stood still for a split second. The man had the most amazing mouth. Firm lips that could caress a woman's breast or kiss her senseless in the space of a heartbeat.

Though it had been two long years, Lucy still remembered the taste of his tongue on hers.

"Jeff?" She heard the impatience in her voice. "I asked you a question."

He nodded slowly. "Okay. Hear me out before you run screaming from the room."

Her nape prickled. "I don't understand."

Leaning toward her, he rested his forearms on the table, hands clasped in front of him. His dark gaze captured hers like a mesmerist. "When you walked out the night before our wedding, we never had closure. I went from being almost married to drastically single so fast it's a wonder I didn't get whiplash."

"What's your point?" Her throat was tight.

"Divorced couples end up back in bed together all the time. Lovers break up and hook up and break up again. I'm curious to see if you and I still have a spark."

Hyperventilation threatened. "We can talk about that later." *Much later.* "You said you had two conditions. What are they?" For the first time tonight, she caught a glimpse of something in his eyes. Was it pain? Or vulnerability? Not likely.

He shrugged. "I want you to ask Kirsten to tell you what really happened that night."

"I don't need to talk to Kirsten. I'm not blind. I saw everything. You kissed her and she kissed you back. Both of you betrayed me. The truth is, Kirsten and I have barely spoken since that night. She has shut me out. I think she's embarrassed that she didn't stop you."

"And you really believe that?"

His tone wasn't sarcastic. If anything, the words were wistful, cajoling. She'd spent two horrid years wondering why the man who professed to love her madly had been such a jerk. Or why Kirsten, her best friend, hadn't punched Jeff in the stomach. She had seen Kirsten's face when Lucy caught them. The other woman had looked shattered. But her arms had definitely been twined about Jeff's neck.

"I don't know what to believe anymore," she muttered. Jeff hadn't dated anyone at all in the last twenty-four months according to Royal's gossipy grapevine. He was a young, virile man in his prime. If he was such a lying, cheating scoundrel, why hadn't he been out on the town with a dozen women in the interim? "And if I do go talk to Kirsten about what happened? That's it? What about the other requirement?"

Those chiseled lips curved upward in a smile that made her spine tighten and her stomach curl. "I'd like the two of us to go upstairs and spend the night together."

Eleven

Go upstairs and spend the night together.

His words echoed in her brain like tiny pinballs. "You mean sex?"

Jeff laughed out loud, but it was gentle laughter, and his eyes were filled with warmth. "Yes, Lucy. Sex. I've missed you. I've missed us."

Oh, my...

What was a woman supposed to say to that kind of proposition? Especially when it sounded so very appealing. She cleared her throat. "If you're offering to pay me twenty thousand dollars to have sex with you, I think we could both get arrested."

His smile was enigmatic. "Let's not muddy the waters, then. I promise to give you the money for Kenny as long as you have a conversation with Kirsten." He reached across the table and took one of her hands in both of his. When he rubbed his thumb across her wrist, it was all she could do not to jerk away in a panic.

"Steady, Lucy." His grip tightened. "I think deep in your heart you know the truth. But you're afraid to face it. I understand that. Maybe it will take time. So for tonight, I'm not expecting you to make any sweeping declarations. I'm only asking if you'll be my lover again. One night. For closure. Unless you change your mind and decide you want more."

"Why would I do that?" she asked faintly, remembering all the evenings she had cried herself to sleep.

"You'll have to figure it out for yourself," he said. That same thumb rubbed back and forth across her knuckles.

She seized on one inescapable truth. "But I don't have anything with me to stay overnight," she said, grasping at straws. "And neither do you."

"I brought a bag," he replied calmly. "And I ordered a few items for a female companion. I believe you'll find I've thought of everything you need to be comfortable."

"And you don't think this is at all creepy?" With her free hand she picked up her water glass, intending to take a sip. But her fingers shook so much she set it back down immediately.

Jeff released her, his expression sober. "You're the one who came to see me, not the other way around. If you want me to take you home, all you have to do is say so. But I'm hoping you'll give us this one night to see if the spark is still there."

"Why are you doing this?" she whispered. He was breaking her heart all over again, and she was so damned afraid to trust him. Even worse, she was afraid to trust herself.

Jeff summoned the waiter and dealt with the check. Moments later, the transaction was complete. Jeff stood and held out his hand. "I need your decision, Lucy." He was tall and sexy and clear-eyed in his resolve. "Shall we go, or shall we stay? It's up to you. It always has been."

Twelve

Jeff's heartbeat thundered in his chest. He wasn't usually much of a gambler, but he was betting on a future that, at the moment, didn't exist.

It was a thousand years before Lucy slid her small hand into his bigger one. "Yes," she said. The word was barely audible.

He led her among the crowded tables and out into the hotel foyer. After tucking her into an elegant wingback chair, he brushed a finger across her cheek. "Stay here. I won't be long."

Perhaps the desk clerk thought him a tad weird. Jeff could barely register for glancing back over his shoulder to see if Lucy had bolted. But all was well. She had her phone in her hand and was apparently checking messages.

When he had the key, he went back for her. "Ready?"

Her face was pale when she looked up at him. But she smiled and rose to her feet. "Yes."

They shared an elevator with three other people. On

the seventh floor, Jeff took Lucy's arm and steered her off. "This way," he said gruffly as he located their room number on the brass placard. They were at the end of the hall, far from the noise of the elevator and the ice machine.

He'd booked a suite. Inside the pleasantly neutral sitting room, he took off his jacket and tie. "Would you like more wine?" he asked.

Lucy hovered by the door. "No. Why do you want me to go talk to Kirsten?" Her eyes were huge…perhaps revealing distress over the shambles of their past.

He leaned against the arm of the sofa. "She was your friend from childhood. You and I had dated less than a year. As angry as I was with you, on some level I understood."

"Why were you angry with *me*?" she asked, her expression bewildered. "You were the one who cheated."

He didn't rise to the bait. "It's been two years, Lucy. Two long, frustrating years when you and I should have been starting our life together. Surely you've had time enough to figure it out by now."

"You didn't come after me." Her voice was small, the tone wounded.

Ah…there it was. The evidence of his own stupidity. "You're right about that. I let my pride get in the way. When you wouldn't take my calls, I wanted to make you grovel. But as it turns out, that was an abysmally arrogant and unproductive attitude on my part. I'm sorry I didn't follow you back to Austin. I should have. Maybe one good knock-down, drag-out fight would have cleared the air."

"And now…if I agree to go talk to Kirsten?"

He swallowed the last of his wine and set the glass aside. "I don't want to discuss Kirsten anymore. You and I are the only two people here in this suite. What I desperately need is make love to you."

Thirteen

Lucy sucked in a deep breath, her insides tumbling as they had the one and only time she rode the Tilt-A-Whirl at the county fair. On that occasion, she had tossed her cookies afterward.

Tonight was different. Tonight, the butterflies were all about anticipation and arousal and the rebirth of hope. Why else would she be here with Jeff Hartley?

She nodded, kicking off her shoes. "Yes." There were a million words she wanted to say to him, and not all of them kind. But for some reason, the only thing that mattered at this very moment was feeling the warmth of his skin beneath her fingers one more time.

She felt more emotionally bereft than brave, but she made her feet move…carrying her across the plush carpet until she stood face-to-face with Jeff. His gaze was stormy, his fists were clenched at his sides.

He stared into her eyes as if looking for something he was afraid he wouldn't find. "God, you're beautiful," he said, his voice hoarse. "I thought I could put you out of my mind, but that was laughable. You've haunted every room in my house. Kiss me, Lucy."

With one of his strong arms around her back, binding her to him, she went up on her tiptoes and found his mouth with hers. The taste of him brought tears to sting her eyelids, but she blinked them back, wanting this moment to be about light and warmth and pleasure. He held her gently as he took everything she thought she knew and stripped it away, leaving only a yearning that was heart-deep and visceral.

She wanted to say something, but Jeff was a man possessed. He found the zipper at her back and lowered it with one smooth move. Then he shimmied the garment down her body and held her arm as she stepped out of the small heap of fabric.

Beneath the dress, she wore lacy underthings. Jeff didn't pause to admire them. The lingerie went the way of the crumpled dress.

Suddenly, she realized that she was completely naked, and her would-be lover was staring. Hotly. Glassy-eyed. As if he'd been struck in the head and was seeing stars.

She crossed her arms over strategic areas and scowled. "Take off your clothes, Mr. Hartley. This show works both ways."

If the situation hadn't been so emotionally fraught, she might have chuckled when Jeff dragged his shirt, still half-buttoned, over his head. His pants and socks and shoes were next in the frenzied disrobing.

Underneath, he wore snug-fitting black boxers that strained to contain his arousal. Suddenly, she felt shy and afraid and clueless. Had she ever really known this man at all?

He didn't give her time for second thoughts. "We'll be more comfortable on the bed," he promised, scooping her up and carrying her through the adjacent doorway. She barely noticed the furnishings or the color scheme. Her gaze was locked on Jeff's face.

His cheekbones were slashed with color. His eyes glittered with lust. "You're mine, Lucy."

Fourteen

The bottom dropped out of her stomach. It was as simple as that. Even if he hadn't said the words, she would have felt his deep conviction in the way he moved his hands over her body.

He still wore his underwear, maybe to keep things from rushing along too rapidly. He was tanned all over from his days of working in the hot sun. His chest was a work of art, sleekly muscled…lightly dusted with golden hair.

Even as she took in the magnificence that was Jeff Hartley, she couldn't help but question his motives. As a rancher and a member of the Texas Cattleman's Club in Royal, he was a well-respected member of the community. Had his reputation suffered when she walked out on him? Was there a part of him that wanted revenge?

He loomed over her on one elbow, his emerald eyes darker than normal, his forehead damp, his skin hot. It was all she could do to be still and let him map her curves like a blind man. Need rose, hot and tormenting, between her clenched thighs.

How could she want him so desperately while knowing full well there were serious unresolved issues between them? "Jeff," she whispered, not really knowing what to say. "Please…" Despite what her head told her, her heart and her body were in control.

It was as if they had never been apart. He rolled her to her stomach and moved aside a swath of her hair to kiss the nape of her neck. The press of his lips against sensitive skin sent sparkles of sensation all down to her feet.

When he nibbled his way along her spine, her hands grabbed the sheets. He lay heavy against her, his big body weighing her down deliciously.

At last she felt him move away. He scrambled out of his boxers and rolled her to face him once again. She let her arms fall lax above her head, enjoying the way his avid gaze scoured her from head to toe.

It had been two years since she had seen him naked… two years since she had seen him at all. Beginning with what would have been their wedding morning, he had phoned her every single day for a week. Each one of those times she had let his call go to voice mail, telling herself he should have had the guts to face her in person.

Had she wronged him grievously? In her blind hurt, had she rushed to judgment? The enormity of the question made her head spin.

For weeks and months, she had wallowed in her self-righteous anger, calling Jeff Hartley every dirty name in the book, telling herself she hated him…that he was a worthless cad, a two-timing player.

But what if she had been wrong? What if she had been terribly, dreadfully wrong?

He used his thumb to erase the frown lines between her brows. "What's the matter, buttercup?"

Hearing the silly nickname made the lump in her throat grow larger. "I don't know what we're doing, Jeff."

His smile was lopsided, more rueful than happy. "Damned if I know either. But let's worry about that tomorrow."

She cupped his cheek, feeling the light stubble of late-day beard. "Since when do *you* channel Scarlett O'Hara?"

Without answering, he reached in his discarded pants for a condom and took care of business. Then he moved between her thighs. "Put your arms around my neck, Lucy. I want to feel you skin to skin."

Fifteen

Jeff tried to live an honorable life. He gave to charity, offered work to those who needed it, supported his local civic organizations and donated large sums of money to the church where he had been baptized as an infant.

But lying in Lucy's arms, on the brink of restaking a claim that had lain dormant for two years, he would have sold his soul to the devil if he could have frozen time.

Lucy's eyes were closed.

"Look at me," he commanded. "I want you to see my face when I take you."

Her breath came in short, sharp pants. She nodded, her eyelids fluttering upward as she obeyed.

Gently, he spread her thighs and positioned his aching flesh against the moist, pink lips of her sex. When he pushed inside, he was pretty sure he blacked out for a moment. *Two years. Two damn years.*

It was everything he remembered and more. The fragrance of her silky skin. The sound of her soft, incoherent cries. His body and his soul would have recognized her even in the dark, anywhere in the world.

He felt her heart beating against his chest. Or maybe it was his heart. It was impossible to separate the two. Burying his face in the crook of her shoulder, he moved in her steadily, sucking in a sharp breath when she wrapped her legs around his waist, driving him deeper.

He thrust slowly at first, but all the willpower in the world couldn't stem the tide of his hunger. His body betrayed him, his desire cresting sharply in a release that left him almost insensate.

Lucy hadn't come. He knew that. But his embarrassment was blunted by the sheer euphoria of being with her again. He kissed her cheek. "I'm sorry, love." He touched her gently, intimately, stroking and teasing until she climaxed, too. Afterward, he held her close for long minutes.

But reality eventually intruded.

Lucy reclined on her elbow, head propped on her hand. "May I ask you a very personal question?"

Though his breathing was still far from steady, he nodded. "Anything."

Lucy reached out and smoothed a lock of his hair. Her gaze was troubled. "When was the last time you had sex?"

Here it was. The first test of their tenuous reconciliation. "You should know," he said quietly. "You were there."

She went white, her expression anguished, tears spilling from her eyes and rolling down her cheeks. "You're lying," she whispered.

Her accusation angered him. But he gathered her into his arms and held her as she sobbed. Two years of grief and separation. Two years of lost happiness.

"I know you don't believe me, Lucy." He combed her hair with his fingers. "Maybe you never will. Don't cry so hard. You'll make yourself sick."

Perhaps they should have talked first. But his need for

her had obliterated everything else. Now she was distraught, and he didn't know how to help her get to the truth. Was this going to be the only moment they had? If so, he wasn't prepared to let it end so soon.

Feeling her nude body against his healed the raw places inside him. She was his. He would fight. For however long it took. No matter what happened, he was never letting her go again.

Sixteen

Lucy's brain whirled in sickening circles. Jeff wanted her to believe he hadn't been with another woman since she walked out on him. He expected her to believe he had not cheated on her.

She should have been elated…relieved. Instead, she was shattered and confused and overwhelmed. Was she going to be one of those women who blindly accepted whatever her lover told her? Where was her pride? Her intuition? Her intellect?

Jeff was silent, but tense. She knew him well enough to realize that he was angry. Even so, the strong arms holding her close were her only anchors at a moment when everything she thought she knew was shattering into tiny fragments and swirling away.

At last, the storm of grief passed. She lay against him limp with emotional distress. Taking a deep breath, she tried to sit up. "We need to go back to Royal. Right now. I need to see you and Kirsten in the same room at the same time to hash this out."

Jeff moved up against the headboard. His jaw was tight, but he scooped her into his lap. "It can wait until tomorrow. We deserve this night together, Lucy. You and I. No one else. Even if you don't believe me."

With her cheek against his chest, she seesawed between hope and despair. Was it possible she hadn't lost him after all, or was she being a credulous fool? If she had placed more trust in what they had from the beginning, it might never have come to this. Was it too late to repair the damage and to reclaim the future that had almost been destroyed?

And what if Jeff *had* initiated the kiss with Kirsten? Could she forgive him and move on? Was what they had worth another chance? Would their relationship ever be the same?

She was deeply moved, unbearably regretful, and at the same time giddy with hope. Tipping back her head so she could see his face, she memorized his features. The heavy-lidded green eyes. The strong chin. The slightly crooked nose. The tiny scar below his left cheekbone.

He gazed down at her with a half-smile. "Are we good?"

"I'm not sure." She wanted to say more. She wanted to pour out her heart…to tell him about the endless months of despair and loneliness. But now was not the time to be sad. "Kiss me again," she whispered unsteadily. "So I know this isn't a dream."

Jeff leaned her over his arm and gave her what she asked for, warm and slow…soft and deep. With each fractured sigh on her part and every ragged groan from him, arousal shimmered and spread until every cell of her body pulsed wildly with wanting him. She grabbed handfuls of his hair, trying to drag him closer.

He winced and laughed. "Easy, darlin'. I don't want to go bald just yet."

His trademark humor was one of the things that had attracted her to him in the beginning. That and his broad-shouldered, lanky body.

Before she knew what was happening, he had levered her onto her back and was leaning over her, shaping the curves of her breasts with his fingertips. Her nipples were so sensitive, she could hardly stand for him to touch them.

"I need you inside me again," she pleaded.

"Not yet." His smile was feral. "Have patience, Lucy, love. We've got all night."

Seventeen

Jeff wanted to worship her body and mark it as his and drive her insane with pleasure. It was a tall order for a man still wrung out from his own release. Not that he wasn't ready for another round. He was. He definitely was. His erection throbbed with a hunger that wouldn't be sated anytime soon.

But somehow he had to make Lucy understand.

When he tasted the tips of her breasts, circled the areolas with his tongue, she gasped and arched her back. He pressed her to the mattress and moved south, teasing her belly button before kissing his way down her hips and thighs and legs one at a time. He even spent a few crazy minutes playing with her toes, and this from a man who had never once entertained a foot fetish.

By this point, she was calling him names...pleading for more.

He laughed, but it was a hoarse laugh. He knew the joke was on him. All his plans to demonstrate how high he could push her evaporated in the driving urge to fill her and erase the memory of every hour that had separated them.

His brain was so fuzzy he only remembered the new condom at the last minute. Once he was ready, he knelt and lifted one of Lucy's legs onto his shoulder. He paused— only a moment—to appreciate the sensual picture she made.

Everything about her was perfect...from the graceful arch of her neck to her narrow waist to the small mole just below her right breast.

He touched her deliberately, stroking the little spot that made her body weep for him. Even though he was gentle and almost lazy in his caress, Lucy climaxed wildly, her release beautiful and real and utterly impossible to resist. "God, I want you," he muttered.

When he thrust inside her, her orgasm hit another peak. The feel of her inner muscles fluttering against his sex drove him to the brink of control. He went still...chest heaving, hips moving restlessly despite his pause.

"Lucy?"

Her teeth dug into her bottom lip. "Yes?"

"I was furious with you for not trusting me. But I never stopped loving you."

"Oh, Jeff..." The look on her face told him she wasn't there yet. She still had doubts. He could wait, maybe. He wanted her to be absolutely sure. For now it was enough to feel...and to know...

Lucy was his.

He retreated and lifted her onto her knees, stuffing pillows beneath her. Her butt was the prettiest thing he'd ever seen, heart-shaped and full. Lucy had bemoaned the curves of her bottom on numerous occasions. Tonight, as he palmed it and squeezed it and steadied himself against it to enter her again with one firm push, he decided he could spend the rest of his life proving to her how perfect it was.

Leaning forward, he gathered her hair into a ponytail, securing it with his fist and using the grip to turn her head. "Look in the mirror, Lucy. This is us. This is real."

Eighteen

Lucy hadn't even noticed that the dresser was conveniently situated across from the bed…and that the mirror faithfully reflected Jeff's sun-bronzed body and her own paler frame. The carnal image was indelibly imprinted on her brain. As long as she lived, she would never forget this moment.

She closed her eyes and bent her head. Jeff released her hair, letting it fall around her face. Behind her, his harsh breathing was audible. At last, he moved with a muffled shout, slamming into her again and again until he shuddered and moaned and slumped on top of her as they both collapsed onto the mattress.

Minutes later…maybe hours, so skewed was her sense of time, she stirred. In the interim, they had untangled their bodies. Jeff lay flat on his back, one arm flung across his eyes. She snuggled against him, draping her leg across his hairy thigh. "Are you alive?"

"Mmph…"

It wasn't much of a response, but it made her smile.

She danced her fingertips over his rib cage. At one time, he had been very ticklish.

His face scrunched up and he batted her hand away. "Five minutes," he begged, the words slurred. "That's all I need."

"Take your time," she teased. She rested her cheek against his chest, feeling so light with happiness it was a wonder she didn't float up to the ceiling. Maybe she was being naive. Maybe he would hurt her again. But at the moment, none of that seemed to matter.

"You never gave me a chance to explain two years ago," he muttered.

His statement dampened her euphoria. "Would it have mattered? I was desperately hurt and in shock. I'm not sure anything you said would have gotten through to me."

"I deserved a fair hearing, Lucy. We were in a committed relationship, but you were too stubborn to be reasonable."

His eyes were closed, so she couldn't see his expression. But his jaw was tight.

Was it all an act? Jeff playing up his innocence?

There was only one way to know for sure, even if the prospect curled her stomach. "Will you do me a favor?" she asked quietly.

Jeff yawned. "The way I feel right now, you could ask me for the moon and I'd call NASA to help me get it for you."

She reared up on one elbow and gaped. "Why, Jeff Hartley! That was the most romantic thing you've ever said to me."

And there it was again. *Doubt.* Many a woman had been swayed by pretty words.

He chuckled, holding her tightly against his side. "I've had two years to practice," he said. "Prepare to be amazed.

But let's not get off track. What's this big favor you need from me?"

"Will you go with me to Kirsten's house?"

His entire body froze. "If it's all the same to you, I'd rather not come anywhere near that woman."

She kissed his bicep. "Please. I have to hear the truth. I know you want me to take you on faith, but I need something more concrete. I need you to understand my doubts, and I need your moral support."

"Damn it. That's what I get for promising you the moon."

Nineteen

The following morning when Lucy woke up, she didn't know where she was. And then it all came back to her in a rush of memories from the night before. She and Jeff Hartley had done naughty things in this huge bed. Naughty, wonderful things.

During the night, he had insisted on holding her close as they slept, though in truth, sleep had been far down the list of their favorite activities. Actually, ranking right below mind-blowing sex were the strawberries and champagne they had ordered from room service at 3:00 a.m.

Jeff was still asleep. She studied him unashamedly, feeling her heart swell with hope and then contract with fear. Loving him once had nearly destroyed her. Could she let herself love him again?

She flinched in surprise when the naked man beneath the covers moved and spoke. "I am not a peep show for your private entertainment," he mumbled.

Reaching beneath the sheet, she took him in her hand. "Are you sure?"

What followed was a very pleasant start to their morning. When they were both rumpled and limp with satisfaction, she poked his arm. "Time to put on some clothes and check out. I want to get this over with."

An hour later, they were on the highway, headed back to Royal. Lucy sat rigid in her seat, her hands clenched in her lap. Layers of dread filled her stomach with each passing mile.

When they reached the fringes of Royal proper, Jeff pulled off on the side of the road and turned to face her. "There's something else I need to tell you."

She blanched. "Oh?"

"Nothing bad," he said hastily, correctly reading her state of mind. "I want you to know that I had my bank transfer twenty thousand dollars to Kenny's account before you and I ever made it to Midland. I wanted you and me to be intimate, but only if you wanted it, too."

Lucy shook her head. "Thank you for that." But even as she said the words, she wondered if his generosity might be a ploy to win her trust…to play the knight in shining armor.

Of course, Jeff knew where Kirsten lived. The party where Jeff and Lucy first connected had been down the street from Kirsten's house. When Jeff parked at the curb, Lucy took a deep breath. "This is it, I guess."

Jeff was at her side as they made their way up the walk. Lucy rang the bell. Kirsten herself opened the door…and upon seeing Lucy and Jeff together, immediately turned the color of milk, her expression distraught. She didn't invite them in. They stood in an awkward trio with the noonday sun beaming down.

Lucy squared her shoulders. "It's been painful having you treat me so coldly these last two years, Kirsten. But

I have to know the truth. If Jeff kissed you and you were seduced into responding, I need to hear you admit it."

Kirsten scowled. "What does the sainted Jeff Hartley have to say about the whole mess? I suppose he's told you what a bitch I am...what a terrible friend."

"Actually, he hasn't said much of anything. The man I knew two years ago wouldn't have cheated on me. But the only other explanation is that my best friend deliberately ruined my wedding."

Kirsten wrapped her arms around her waist, her expression hunted. "Why would I do that?"

"I don't know. But I've run out of scenarios, and I'm damned tired of wondering." Kirsten sneered. "Men are pigs. They want what they can't have. Jeff put the moves on me. He cheated on you."

Suddenly, the pain was as fresh as if the incident had happened yesterday. Seeing Kirsten in Jeff's arms had nearly killed Lucy. But now she had to take one of them on faith. Either her childhood friend or her lover.

She stared at Kirsten. "Did *he* cheat on me? Or did *you*?"

It was a standoff two years in the making. No matter what the answer turned out to be, Lucy lost someone she cared about, someone she loved.

Jeff remained silent during the long, dreadful seconds that elapsed. Time settled into slow motion...

At last, Kirsten's face crumpled. Her eyes flashed with a combination of guilt and anger. "If you'd had more faith in him, nothing I did would have mattered."

Lucy gasped, struck by the truth in the accusation. But her own behavior wasn't on trial at the moment. Shock paralyzed her, despite the part of her that must have accepted the truth somewhere deep down inside. "So it's true?" Lucy spared one glance at Jeff, but he was stone-faced.

Kirsten shrugged. "It's true. Your precious Jeff is innocent."

Lucy trembled. Knowing was one thing. Hearing it bluntly stated out loud was painful...and baffling. "Why, Kirsten? I have to know why?"

Kirsten was almost defiant now. "I was jealous. Ever since we were kids, things seemed so easy for you. When we came back from college and you hooked up with Jeff at the party, I was furious. I'd had my eye on him for a long time."

Lucy shook her head in disbelief. "You were so popular, Kirsten. I don't even know what you mean."

Kirsten shrugged. "I hoarded my resentment. Everything came to a head the night of your rehearsal dinner. I saw my chance and I took it. I kissed Jeff. Because I knew you were right outside the door. He had nothing to do with it."

"Oh, Kirsten. You were my best friend."

The other woman shook her head. "But not anymore." Quietly, Kirsten closed the door.

Twenty

Jeff took Lucy's arm and steered her back toward the car. "Give her time," he said. "The two of you may get beyond this."

Lucy stared at him. "How can you be so calm?"

He caressed her cheek, his eyes filled with warmth. "I have you back in my life again, Lucy. Nothing can hurt me now."

"Take me home with you, Jeff. Please."

They made the trip in silence. Her thoughts were in shambles. How had she been so wrong about so many things?

In Jeff's living room, she prowled. He leaned a shoulder against the doorframe, his gaze following her around the room. At last, he sighed. "Sometimes we have to put the past behind us, sweetheart. We have to choose to be happy and move on."

At last, Lucy stood in front of him, hands on her hips.

"I love you, too, Jeff. I'm sorry I didn't trust you…that I didn't trust us. Kirsten had been my friend since we were nine years old. When I saw her in your arms, it didn't make sense. So my default was to doubt you. And maybe to doubt myself, too, because I fell in love with you so quickly." She took a deep breath. "I adore you. I suppose I'll have to spend the rest of my life making this up to you."

He pulled her close and kissed her hard, making her heart skip several beats. "Nonsense. We're not going to talk about it again. Today is our new beginning."

Even in the midst of an almost miraculous second chance, Lucy fretted. "There's one more thing."

He scooped her into his arms and carried her to the sofa, sprawling with her in his arms. "Go ahead," he said, his tone resigned.

"I don't want people to gossip about us. Can we please keep this quiet? At least until after Christmas? That will give me time to go back to Austin and turn in my notice. I'll have to sell my condo if I'm coming back to run the farm. I'll convince Kenny to turn down the Samson Oil offer and stick around until the new year."

Jeff's eyes narrowed…giving him the look of a really pissed off cowboy. "No way," he said, his jaw thrust out. "We're getting married this week. I'm not stupid."

She petted his shirtfront. "Then go with me to Austin," she said urgently. "We'll have a quiet wedding at the courthouse. Just you and me. But nobody has to know. I want time for us to be us." She kissed his chin. "You understand, don't you?"

He moved her beneath him on the sofa, unzipping her black pants and toying with the lacy edge of her undies. "As long as you're in my bed every night, I'll do whatever you want, Lucy. But I won't wait to put my ring on your finger."

She linked her arms around his neck, drawing his head down so she could kiss him. "Whatever you say, cowboy. I'm all yours."

* * * * *

Don't miss a single installment of
TEXAS CATTLEMAN'S CLUB:
LIES AND LULLABIES

*Baby secrets and a scheming
sheikh rock Royal, Texas*

*If you're on Twitter, tell us what you think
of Harlequin Desire! #harlequindesire*

COMING NEXT MONTH FROM

⬡ HARLEQUIN®

Desire

Available December 1, 2015

#2413 BANE
The Westmorelands • by Brenda Jackson
Rancher and military hero Bane Westmoreland is on a mission to reconnect with the one who got away—his estranged wife. And when the beautiful chemist's discovery puts her in danger, Bane vows to protect her at all costs...

#2414 TRIPLETS UNDER THE TREE
Billionaires and Babies • by Kat Cantrell
A plane crash took his memory. But then billionaire fighter Antonio Cavallari makes it home for the holidays only to discover the triplets he never knew...and their very off-limits, very tempting surrogate mother.

#2415 LONE STAR HOLIDAY PROPOSAL
Texas Cattleman's Club: Lies and Lullabies
by Yvonne Lindsay
At risk of losing her business, single mother Raina Patterson finds solace in the arms of Texas deal-maker Nolan Dane. But does this mysterious stranger have a hidden agenda that will put her heart at even bigger risk?

#2416 A WHITE WEDDING CHRISTMAS
Brides and Belles • by Andrea Laurence
When a cynical wedding planner is forced to work with her teenage crush to plan his sister's Christmas wedding, sparks fly! But will she finally find a happily-ever-after of her own with this second-chance man?

#2417 THE RANCHER'S SECRET SON
Lone Star Legends • by Sara Orwig
For wealthy rancher Nick Milan, hearing the woman he loved and lost tell him he's a daddy is the shock of a lifetime. The revelation could derail his political career...or put the real prize back within tantalizing reach...

#2418 TAKING THE BOSS TO BED
by Joss Wood
After producer Ryan Jackson kisses a stranger to save her from his client's unwanted attentions, he realizes she's actually his newest employee! Faking a relationship is now essential for business, but soon real passion becomes the bottom line...

With her heart thundering hard in her chest, Crystal
began throwing items in the suitcase open on her bed.
Had she imagined it or had she been watched when she'd
entered her home tonight? She had glanced around several
times and hadn't noticed anything or anyone. But still…

She took a deep breath, knowing she couldn't lose her
cool. She made a decision to leave her car here and a few
lights burning inside her house to give the impression she
was home. She would call a cab to take her to the airport
and would take only the necessities and a few items of
clothing. She could buy anything else she needed.

But this, she thought as she studied the photo album
she held in her hand, went everywhere with her. She had
purchased it right after her last phone call with Bane.
Her parents had sent Crystal to live with Aunt Rachel to
finish out the last year of school. They wanted to get her
away from Bane, not knowing she and Bane had secretly
married.

A couple of months after she left Denver, she'd gotten
a call from him. He'd told her he'd enlisted in the navy

because he needed to grow up, become responsible and make something out of himself. She deserved a man who could be all that he could be, and after he'd accomplished that goal he would come for her. Sitting on the edge of the bed now, she flipped through the album, which she had dedicated to Bane. She thought of him often. Every day. What she tried not to think about was why it was taking him so long to come back for her, or how he might be somewhere enjoying life without her. Forcing those thoughts from her mind, she packed the album in her luggage.

Moments later, she had rolled her luggage into the living room and was calling for a cab when her doorbell rang.

She went still. Nobody ever visited her. Who would be doing so now? She crept back into the shadows of her hallway, hoping whoever was at the door would think she wasn't home. She held her breath when the doorbell sounded again. Did the person on the other side know she was there?

She rushed into her bedroom and grabbed her revolver out of the nightstand drawer. By the time she'd made it back to the living room, there was a second knock. She moved toward the door, but stopped five feet away. "Who is it?" She tightened her hands on the revolver.

There was a moment of silence. And then a voice said, "It's me, Crystal. Bane."

Bane will do whatever it takes to keep his woman safe, but will it be enough?

Don't miss BANE by New York Times bestselling author Brenda Jackson. Available December 2015 wherever Harlequin® Desire books and ebooks are sold.

www.Harlequin.com

HARLEQUIN

Desire

This Christmas, he'll meet his three babies for the first time... and desire their mother in a whole new way!

A plane crash took his memory. But then billionaire fighter Antonio Cavallari makes it home for the holidays only to discover the triplets he never knew...and their very off-limits, very tempting surrogate mother.

Triplets Under the Tree is part of Harlequin Desire's #1 bestselling series, **Billionaires and Babies**: Powerful men... wrapped around their babies' little fingers.

SAVE $1.00

on the purchase of TRIPLETS UNDER THE TREE by Kat Cantrell {available Dec. 1, 2015} or any other Harlequin® Desire book.

Redeemable at participating outlets in the U.S. and Canada only. Not redeemable at Barnes & Noble stores. Limit one coupon per customer.

52613164

Canadian Retailers: Harlequin Enterprises Limited will pay the face value of this coupon plus 10.25¢ if submitted by customer for this product only. Any other use constitutes fraud. Coupon is nonassignable. Void if taxed, prohibited or restricted by law. Consumer must pay any government taxes. Void if copied. Millenium1 Promotional Services ("M1P") customers submit coupons and proof of sales to Harlequin Enterprises Limited, P.O. Box 3000, Saint John, NB E2L 4L3, Canada. Non-M1P retailer—for reimbursement submit coupons and proof of sales directly to Harlequin Enterprises Limited, Retail Marketing Department, 225 Duncan Mill Rd., Don Mills, Ontario M3B 3K9, Canada.

5 65373 00076 2 (8100)0 12107

U.S. Retailers: Harlequin Enterprises Limited will pay the face value of this coupon plus 8¢ if submitted by customer for this product only. Any other use constitutes fraud. Coupon is nonassignable. Void if taxed, prohibited or restricted by law. Consumer must pay any government taxes. Void if copied. For reimbursement submit coupons and proof of sales directly to Harlequin Enterprises Limited, P.O. Box 880478, El Paso, TX 88588-0478, U.S.A. Cash value 1/100 cents.

COUPON EXPIRES JAN. 4, 2016

Available wherever books are sold, including most bookstores, supermarkets, drugstores and discount stores.

www.Harlequin.com

HDCOUP1115